COMFORT FOOD FOR THE SOUL...

FRIENDSHIP CAKE

Warm and tender, this unforgettable tale
of togetherness and resilience offers every woman
the recipes from which good food—
and good living—are made.

Comfort food for the soul . . .

Friendship Cake

Warm and tender, this unforgettable tale of togetherness and resilience offers every woman the recipes from which good food—and good living—are made.

———◦◦◦———

"Mix up two parts *Steel Magnolias*, one part *Fried Green Tomatoes*, and a dash of Mitford, and you've got *Friendship Cake* . . . the perfect summertime read."

ANGIE HOWARD, DAVIS–KIDD BOOKSELLERS,

NASHVILLE, TENNESSEE

"Hinton's characters seem as real as the nearest church group or book club, and they all season this stew to perfection. An eclectic collection of tantalizing Southern recipes is a real bonus."

ROCKY MOUNTAIN NEWS

―――――◦◦◦◦◦―――――

"I couldn't decide which to do first— finish the beautiful story, or try my hand at one of the recipes."

TERESA PREGNALL, AUTHOR OF

TREASURED RECIPES FROM THE CHARLESTON CAKE LADY

―――――◦◦◦◦◦―――――

"Hinton has done a masterful job using recipes as a structural device for her novel. Hinton has also done an admirable job creating complex and diverse characters. Her experiences as a pastor and hospice chaplain allow her to tell a story with frankness, grace and humor."

NEWS AND RECORD NEWSPAPER (GREENSBORO, NC)

Available in Hardcover

THE THINGS I KNOW BEST

FRIENDSHIP CAKE

LYNNE HINTON

HarperTorch
*An Imprint of HarperCollins*Publishers*

This is a work of fiction. Names, characters, places, and incidents are products of the author's imagination or are used fictitiously and are not to be construed as real. Any resemblance to actual events, locales, organizations, or persons, living or dead, is entirely coincidental.

❦

HARPERTORCH
An Imprint of HarperCollins*Publishers*
10 East 53rd Street
New York, New York 10022-5299

Copyright © 2000 by Lynne Hinton
ISBN: 0-380-82014-5
Excerpt from *The Things I Know Best* copyright © 2001 by Lynne Hinton

First HarperTorch paperback printing: August 2001
First HarperSanFrancisco hardcover printing: May 2000

HarperCollins ®, HarperTorch™, and ❦ ™ are trademarks of Harper-Collins Publishers Inc.

Printed in the United States of America

Visit HarperTorch on the World Wide Web at www.harpercollins.com

10 9 8 7 6 5 4 3 2 1

for Anna Bess Brown,
truly, completely, undeniably
my friend

Acknowledgments

Recognizing that this book could not have been possible without the support, direction, and love of many people, I gratefully acknowledge my family, who have put up with me a very long time, especially my husband, who loved me even without a publishing contract, and his parents, Charlotte and Eddie; my agent, Sally McMillan, who believed in my stories; my editors, Joann Davis, for saying yes, and Michelle Shinseki, who has made this endeavor such a joy; Sylvia Belvin and Frances Holt from Fran's Front Porch and First Christian Church, Greensboro, North Carolina, for allowing me to use their recipes; Lynn and Edith and Eddie for the cooking advice; Carlene Neese for first explaining the friendship cake tradition to me; Kaye Crawford for "hatch, match, and dispatch"; the women with whom I romp on the first Thursday of every month, Julie, Judy, Peggy, Dorisanne, Terry,

Acknowledgments

Dale, and Jacqueline; and all the other friends who make my life so rich, including Julie, Robin, Melissa, Ronny, Terry and Melanie, Charles, Steve, Katrin, Dave and Ella, Don, and, of course, Tina.

Finally I wish to say thank you to all the folks at Mount Hope United Church of Christ and First Congregational United Church of Christ. From you I have discovered how to recognize and honor grace.

And please note: A portion of the proceeds of this book will go to Hospice of Alamance-Caswell Counties, for here is where I have learned my greatest lessons.

List of Recipes

List of Recipes

MEATS

DESSERTS

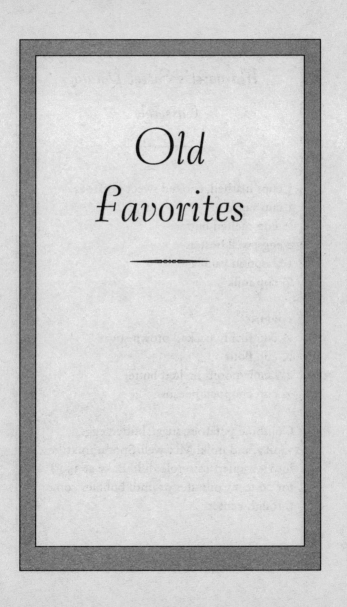

Old Favorites

Margaret's Sweet Potato Casserole

---

3 cups mashed, cooked sweet potatoes
1 cup sugar
½ cup melted butter
2 eggs, well beaten
1 teaspoon vanilla
⅓ cup milk

TOPPING
½ cup firmly packed brown sugar
¼ cup flour
2½ tablespoons melted butter
¾ cup chopped pecans

Combine potatoes, sugar, butter, eggs, vanilla, and milk. Mix well. Spoon mixture into a 2-quart casserole dish. Bake at 350°F for 20 to 25 minutes or until bubbles come through center.

Combine topping ingredients, mixing them well, and sprinkle on top of potatoes. Bake 5 minutes more.

—MARGARET PEELE

—

The Cookbook Committee of the Hope Springs
Community Church is currently receiving
recipes for their upcoming Women's Guild
Cookbook. Anyone with recipes please contact one of
the following women: Margaret Peele, Louise Fisher,
Beatrice Newgarden, or Jessie Jenkins.

*T*here. That was short, to the point, and easy to type. Surely, Rev. Stewart wouldn't have a problem printing that in the bulletin. One could never be sure. She likes her announcements worded a certain way. At least four people I know of, personally, have seen their flower memorials and their thank-you notes shortened or added to by this woman pastor who thinks she has a flair for words.

Truth be told, no one really complains about what she does with the announcements, it just seems like a lot of work for a girl who appears not to have any extra time. After all, no one really cares if the flowers are "lovingly placed in memory" or simply "put at the altar." They just want to make sure their mama's name is spelled right and that each of the seven children is listed in correct birth order. Names and dates. That's what matters.

Sometimes I'm not sure the young pastor has a good hold on what really matters; but she tries hard and most of the people are warm to her, so I don't plan to rock her boat by saying such a thing to her. Besides, she's young, she'll learn. We all do.

This cookbook was not my idea. Since the Women's Guild is dying out, we're running out of money. It was Peggy DuVaughn's notion that we needed to raise some money. And then I think it was Beatrice Newgarden, who has nothing better to do than volunteer at the funeral parlor, who agreed we should have a project. Great, I think, a project. Another project. And before I have a chance to write it down in my secretary's notes, it's a cookbook, and I'm in charge.

As far as cooking goes, I'm considered only fair by the women in this community. Out here, everybody grows their own vegetables, has their own livestock, kills, milks, and cans. So every recipe begins with something like "Strip all the feathers from the bird" or "Make sure the roots and stems are cut." The standards are a little higher than say, Greensboro, where I took my sweet potato casserole to a women's meeting; and having set it down next to all the KFC boxes and the Winn-Dixie potato salad, was treated like I was Cordelia Kelly from Channel 2's cooking show.

Here, in the county, women grew up learning to cook before they were tall enough to reach the stove. It was the mother's and the grandmother's responsibility to make sure all the girls in the family could make a meal out of one strip of meat and a cup of beans. So we learned to cook. And we learned to be creative. We learned how to stretch dough across two weeks at three squares a day. We learned how to make soup from bones and old potatoes. And we learned to knead our sorrows and our dreams into loaves of bread and our worthiness into cherry pies and fatty pork chops.

When my mama died and I was ten, I lost interest in what the female gender does in the kitchen. My older sisters cooked and cleaned while I worked in the fields, on the tractor, and behind the woodshed. I did anything that kept me from standing in my mama's prints that were worn into the boards in front of the sink or cast in iron in the handles of skillets. Those days folks didn't know what to do with a grieving child, so they just let me do the work of men and left me to myself.

My daddy was solemn, not much with words or girl children. But because I looked the most like my mother and because I stayed as close to him as the film of dirt that crept from the fields into wrinkles and under nails, he paid me the most attention. I pretended for a very long time that my sisters and brothers didn't notice, but after he died I sensed the resentment and the stones of sibling rivalry as they pelted me with their grief-stricken stares.

I was, after all, the only one he would let shave him or feed him teaspoonsful of honey. His last five years he lived with each daughter and son, but everyone knew that he was saving my house for last. Like getting ready for retirement, Daddy mapped out his final six months with great care. When he left Woodrow's to enter the hospital for the eighth time, he sent his belongings to me, and, leaving the cancer unit, Daddy came home to 516 Hawthorne Lane to die.

Surely he knew that I was the only one who would pick him up and set him behind the wheel of the tractor, wait until the vomiting stopped, and then steer him across the pasture while he worked the pedals. I was the only one who would pad down the dirt and make a hard path so that I could push his wheelchair through the soybean field. I was the only child of his who would not mind hearing his stories over and over, help him reorder his memories, or who would sit with him through thunderstorms while he called me "Mama." So if Beulah and Bessie, Thomas Jack and Woodrow are still mad at me for picking out the casket and telling the funeral director how to dress Daddy, then they are the ones who have to live with anger. All I got is sadness. And a heart can hold sadness a lot longer than it can anger.

I know because I've held both, and the sadness always outlasts the anger. You have to make an intentional decision either to give the anger up or to let it eat out the center of your spirit. Sadness can stay with a body for a lifetime. But with anger, you've got to choose. That's what killed Luther, and that's how I learned such a lesson.

He stayed angry as long as he could. And finally his head exploded because of the clogged pathways from his heart. It had nothing to do with cigarettes or cholesterol like the doctors said and everything to do with anger. I am not sure how it all began. Whether he had the seed of madness in his soul from when he was a boy or whether it was planted when he saw the first construction sign about the hatchery in Eleanor Littleton's hayfield. However it got there, bit by bit, the seed grew inside him so that each time the hatchery sold chickens at a better price or every winter when a storm blew off siding or froze our birds, his face got redder and redder, and the anger welled up in his veins.

I begged him, I pleaded with him, "Give up the chicken farm!" I knew that we both could find public work, but it became an obsession, a war in his mind, and he would not let it go. He died at the age of forty-seven, burying what was left of the carcasses of twenty-five chickens, killed by a pack of wild dogs. The hatchery gave me a fair price for his last shipment of chicks. And even though his brothers and sisters couldn't believe that I'd sell them, and especially to the place that everyone said brought my husband down, I took the money and two years later went on a cruise. Now all that stands as a memorial to that which he would not let go is a fallen down barn surrounded by a steel fence, the pungent odor of old chicken shit, and a few feathers that float just inside the windows.

I live alone. We had no children. I feed five cats and take care of two old dogs. I expect little out of life and am rarely disappointed. I rent out most of the land to Jessie Jenkins's oldest son, who tries to make a go of it every year raising tobacco and corn.

Active in church, I'm chosen to serve on lots of committees. This is partly because folks think I have more time than money and because there is a certain amount of respect granted to women who make it on their own. Unlike Louise Fisher's situation, most people are comfortable with the notion that I'm just a lonely widow and not a homosexual. So that even though we are the same age and in the same economic class, and even though it is common knowledge that Louise knows the Bible better than anyone, I am usually the one asked to chair boards and work on programs.

Nobody knows for sure about Louise. But there are speculations and bits of trashy stories about her car having been discovered at the

Trucker's Lodge Motel and two women's voices coming from room seven; and there is the report on a number of books she receives in the mail from San Francisco.

Frankly, I'm not interested in trashy stories or in the sexual orientation of my friends. And if the truth be told, I am probably a more likely candidate to love a woman than Louise, since I could use a wife to manage the household responsibilities that women are supposedly more inclined to handle. And, at this point in my life, I value more deeply the company of women than men. I think this has to do with the holding of sadness. If forced to choose, women will give up everything else but hold on to that.

I have little energy for anxiety about money or the state of the union. I do love sports but not enough to talk about them, and every evening, just as dusk has passed, I find that I desire the softness of a woman's voice. Though it is my father's voice that rings in my head and all along the edges of my heart, it is the faint and melodic voice of a woman that rocks my soul to sleep.

Most of the women at Hope Springs have never even entertained such a notion. They busy up their lives with the comings and goings of their children and trying to second-guess the needs of their husbands. Their days are filled with talk shows and coupon clipping, malicious gossip about the same women they claim to have as friends, and long gazes into the mirror while they touch the fallen skin along their necks and worry that age will steal it all away.

They are cautious with me because I have little patience for their pettiness. They are civil towards me, however, because they know their husbands admire my fortitude and the way I loved my father. I wouldn't say that they respect me, but they are almost certain to know of my opinion and are guaranteed that I will not bow and curtsy in the way so many of them have been taught.

This unwillingness to cower has occasionally permitted me the surprising opportunity to have long and interesting conversations with daughters and granddaughters who bear great secrets. I would say I am in a most enviable and sacred position. Most of the women in the community know this but would never call attention to it.

For instance, I was the first one to know that Katie Askew was not going to take chemotherapy. A pretty little thing of fifteen and she was diagnosed with a brain tumor. I noticed the shifting of her eyes when she realized that she would lose her long blond curls. Nancy, her mother, was so distraught about the diagnosis and so determined about the treatments that she hadn't even considered that the loss of hair to a fifteen-year-old girl was a fate worse than death. After her first hospitalization, a week before she was to go down to Duke for chemo, Katie had her mother bring her to my house. After her mother left to get her medicines, Katie looked out the window and said, "I want you to talk to my mother."

"About what, Katie?" I asked.

"About the fact that I'm not going to go to Duke for those treatments."

Part of her head was already shaven, but a bandage covered the place behind her left ear. The blond curls fell over it.

"Katie, what makes you think I'd tell your mother such a thing? And, besides, you know that will kill her."

"I remember what you told us in Sunday School four years ago. You said the most important thing is to be honest with the people you love, and if you can't be honest then you should get somebody else to speak your truth. So I'm asking you, will you tell her I'm not going to go?"

The big brown eyes would not let me loose. I tried to find another way. I told her to talk to the preacher or to her father, but little Katie Askew was convinced that I was the messenger of her truth. Finally I told her I would. And true to my word, when Nancy came back and Katie was sleeping in my bed upstairs, I convinced the teenage girl's mother to postpone the treatments until Katie could ease into the idea of queens who wrapped their heads in long, flowing scarves and the open-ended fashion of wearing outrageous straw hats.

Since then I've dealt with everything from failing grades to Penny Throckmorton's plan to elope with a sailor from Norfolk. I'm not altogether comfortable with the role of teenage advocate in the Hope Springs community, but for whatever reason it seems to fit. Besides, all the storms that blow into the lives of families around us funnel the clouds that spin around our own hearts as well.

Like in every community, that's how it goes

here in Hope Springs. Trouble passes from one door to another. Tragedy and adventure not quite as regular, but, still, they come too. And while one mother thanks God for not having sent a particular sorrow her way, she prepares herself for what might be coming next. Because surely every mother knows that when a woman grants life to a new person, a child, sorrow is the only guarantee she will ever have.

Yet even that sometimes sounds better than having to chair every committee or head up every project because all the other women think you're lonely for something to do. Of course, I know I could say no. But I guess I figure I'm luckier than most; I've carried all of the sorrow I'm ever going to have. There isn't much that can break my heart anymore, so I consider it a privilege not to have to worry about the future. And if calling for recipes permits the mothers in this community to spend more energy preparing the soft places in their hearts for hard news, then I'll oblige. Besides, there are worse things to ask for than recipes.

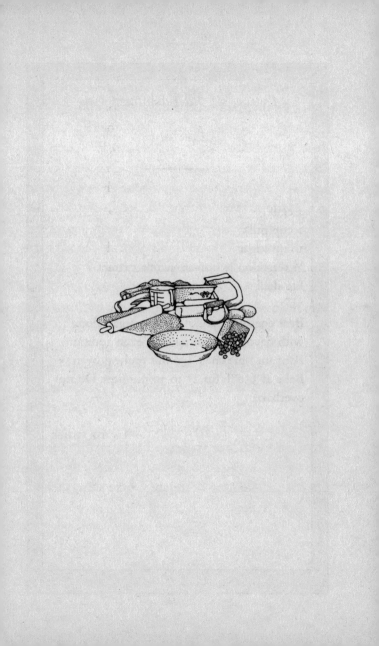

Louise's Old-Fashioned Egg Custard

————∘≻⊶≺∘————

4 eggs
1 cup milk
1 cup sugar
½ teaspoon lemon or vanilla extract
Pie shell

Beat eggs well; add milk and sugar, along
with flavoring, beating after each addition.
Pour into pie shell. Do not preheat oven.
Bake at 350°F for 25 to 30 minutes. Do not
overbake.

—LOUISE FISHER

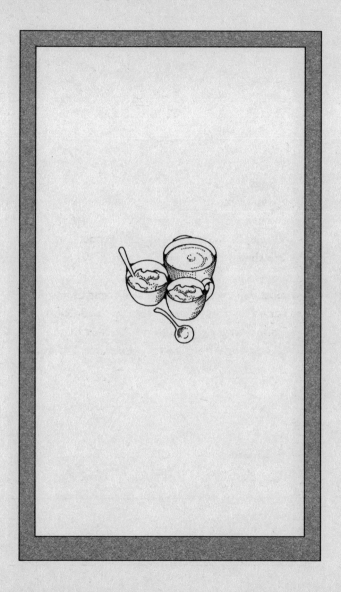

I should have known that it was Beatrice Newgarden who came up with this whole stupid idea of a cookbook. And how did I ever get to be on this committee? Lord knows, neither Margaret nor I can cook. The most I can offer is wieners or burgers, maybe egg custard, the easy version, of course. Everyone knows the fact that we're heading up this committee is a sure sign of failure for this tidy project.

Beatrice is always in need of "binding" us together. It's like a calling for her. Any time she senses a weak link, a friendship in need of something, probably time and space, she assumes she's got to bring people together. She has no sense of boundaries, no sense of where one person, one relationship, ends and where she begins. She's a fairy godmother in a funeral director's suit.

The worst part about it is that she has no idea that she's the poster child for codependency. She's running around sticking her nose up in the air, sniffing for tension or death, and then, like a dog with a bone, she's not going to let the cause alone until she sees breath in that mirror of a face she tries to wear.

It's evident to all the ladies in the church that the Women's Guild has outlived its purpose. But as soon as Beatrice got a whiff of our resignation, she dug up this project as a means to "encourage younger women to join the group" and to "build up the fellowship." I'm surprised she's not been caught trying to resuscitate some of the corpses she dresses. She can't stand to see anything die.

I, on the other hand, joined the Hemlock Society when I was in my forties. I send Dr. Kevorkian a few dollars every month, and I was Hospice Volunteer of the Year two years in a row. I think death is an appropriate answer to the equation of life. I have never seen it as frightful or even poignant. And I certainly do not see it as something to be avoided.

The first death that I remember was my granddaddy Amos, my mother's father. I was seven, and I didn't know him very well since he had been sick since I was three. We lived in his house with my grandmother, but he stayed in a distant room and I rarely saw him. I would make him a card and take him a flower from the garden, but beyond the exchange of those gifts, and the standard prayer for him at bedtime, he was nothing to me.

On the day of his death, my mother, not one to hide things from me, took me into the room before the undertaker came and made me feel his hand and kiss him on the cheek. I know of people who claim they have never been able to touch a dead person since they were made to do so as a child, but it never haunted me. In fact, I was fascinated by the warmth running out of his fingers and the stiffness settling into his wrinkles. It did not seem harsh or terrible to me. It was like going to sleep. And I was never afraid.

Since then, I've buried my grandmother, my mother, and two siblings. You might say that I have developed the reputation for being the deathwatch angel around these parts. I've sat in many a hospital room with dying people because their family couldn't deal with the final hours. I don't mind having this reputation; I consider it a gift. Just like there are some people who can cook and others who weave cloth or build birdhouses, I can sit in a room, watch as death approaches, gently take the hand of the dying person, and lift them in its arms. It's the one thing in my life that I'm sure of.

The rest is a huge question mark. Ambiguous and watery, just like Beatrice's boundaries. And I'm not stupid. I know people are curious about my sexuality. Hell, I'm curious about my sexuality. But I'm sixty-three, and I still do not know what or how it is that I love.

I never married, left home when I was eighteen. I followed my sisters and went to work in a cotton mill just to get away from the farm. There in town I met women whose lives were more cruel than I would ever imagine and men whose hearts were full of greed and malice. I made my home in a boardinghouse with six other young women millworkers, and it was the most of family I have ever really known.

Roxie Ann Barnette and I were roommates. And as well as I can guess, I believe that I fell in love with her. In those days, however, Oprah wasn't around to help you name your relationship. There wasn't any support group to encourage the child within. There were no women running with wolves. Hell, there wasn't even an advice column for girls who had any feelings other than those of desire to raise a family and win a blue ribbon at the state fair. I was confused and lacking in any guidance. So, without complaining, I took the most that I could get, friendship as rich and deep as intimacy can go without touching and a paycheck once a month.

Roxie would set us up on double dates. God bless her for trying. I was even engaged for a brief period. Some man who had his eye on Roxie but settled for her best friend. I can't remember the fellow's name. Anyway, they were lovely, agonizing years of hating myself while trying to fit into somebody else's clothes. Years of not knowing what was wrong with me but feeling certain that I would never be happy. At least once a month I would swear that I was going to move out. It was killing me to be faced with such strange and inappropriate feelings.

To this day, I'm not sure Roxie knows how much I care for her. Never in the four years that we lived together did she seem to know. I could always tell when someone would question her about me; they'd look at me hard while I clung to Roxie's every word. But she never hesitated, never held back. She brushed the accusations and the suspicions aside. She never turned me away. I get the feeling that George, her husband of forty years, knows. There's a bristle to him that apparently only shows up when I'm around. Roxie acts like she doesn't see it. I think I kind of like that, though, that he knows that I could take Roxie to a place just beyond his reach. And she, without hurting either one of us, finds room in her life for us both.

They live in Maryland. I go up to see her every couple of months, and she has frequently come down to see me. We meet at silly motels along the interstate. George prefers that she stay near the highway when she travels. I guess it makes him feel like he can get to her more easily.

She's as beautiful as she was forty-five years ago. Tall and raw-boned, she's a long drink of clear, still water. Dark hair, solid smile. She has eyes like a child. Open, honest. Like her conversations. She's as innocent as rain. The answer to a lonely man's prayers. She believes what you tell her, and she takes everyone at their word.

I'm exactly her antithesis. Short and dumpy

and as muddy as the Mississippi River. And I'm hardly innocent. The only man's prayer I can answer has to do with being able to tote bags of cement twice my body weight and knowing which wrench is used to take off square-headed bolts. And don't expect me to believe anything you say until you prove yourself worthy of my trust. I'm as cynical as I am stubborn, so I rarely get taken advantage of, except by this woman who holds up my heart.

We're about as different as two women can be. But we can finish one another's sentences and wake up with the same dreams. I light the fire and she keeps it going. She tests the ice and I skate behind her. There is nothing I wouldn't do for Roxie. No place I wouldn't travel to find her. No silence I wouldn't hold. I was even her maid of honor, something I swore would never happen on this side of heaven.

When she got married, however, I honored her vows. I respected her relationship with George. But God help me, on their wedding day, hearing the promises, knowing the love that was there and not there, I thought my heart would split. The healing was a long time in coming, and I doubt I'll ever be whole. But I've managed to keep my head about me and not be lost to the emptiness. I've resorted to severe Bible reading, like punishment I suppose, and bonsai gardening. And somehow I find that the two taken in daily doses ease the pain and sharpen my focus. So that the years have passed and I have managed a life, a living, and a livelihood.

I'm the godmother of her two children, been like another grandmother to Ruby's littlest one. So that in some odd sort of old-maid sister kind of role, I've become a part of the family. And much to old George's chagrin, I've found my place in everybody's heart but his.

Recently, I have noticed a change in the way Roxie remembers a story or tries to make a decision. There's a look in her eye that reminds me of the distant daydreaming I used to lose myself in while spinning spools of yarn along big silver bobbins. A step just beyond reality. A pulling of the mind. It's just that it seems she has a harder time getting back.

I was surprised when George called me a month ago to ask if she had written. It seems she was convinced that we were supposed to meet in Virginia the weekend of July Fourth. I knew nothing of these plans but worried that I might spoil some necessary charade she had arranged for herself. So I made up some lie that some of my mail had been missing for a few weeks and could I please speak to her?

"She's not here," he said. There was a long pause, and I knew there was more to be spoken.

"Lou, Roxie isn't well. There was an incident." I remember waiting for more.

"An incident? What the hell does that mean, George?"

He cleared his throat, and I remember thinking it was one of his arrogant but typical gestures. "I've been seeing someone else. For about a year. Rox found out."

I believe my reply was something like "Yeah, that's an incident all right, you son of a bitch. Why is she still with you?"

And he said, "I told you. She isn't well."

I asked him what he meant, and he said that the doctors think she is in the early stages of Alzheimer's. About two years ago they said this.

That's all I remember of that conversation. That and the question of how she could keep such a thing from me. That and the attempt to grasp how I was stupid enough not to see it. All of it, including knowing about the two-timing bastard that she married. I drove up the next day. Roxie seemed surprised and actually quite focused. I asked her if she wanted to come back with me, and she politely refused. We did not speak of the incident.

For three weeks I have called her every day. She will never stay on the phone long enough for me to get a true sense of how she's doing. At least four times she has claimed it's a bad time to talk. And in between phone calls, I find myself vacillating between driving up to Maryland, packing her stuff, and moving her back home with me and staying the hell out of it and letting her handle her own life. I feel like I'm running from Margaret's house to Beatrice's. Ms. Cement-Wall Boundaries to Ms. Floating Borders. I do not know how to be.

I realize that this lifelong struggle, however, is wearing this old heart thin. I know that I cannot tell anyone about this. I understand that it's a secret I do not even know how to tell. I've kept quiet for so long I'm not even sure how to give it words. All I know is that the burden is getting heavier. But it's highly unlikely anybody has any counsel for me now. Too much water beneath the bridge. Too many pages in this chapter.

I suppose I should just keep to the path I've made for myself, fill my time with gardening and the reading of the prophets, the quarterly treat of my bonsai books that come from California, and now this stupid cookbook. Distraction has steadied me this long. Perhaps it will level my thinking a little bit longer.

Beatrice's Prune Cake

---

1 cup salad oil
2 cups sugar
3 eggs
1 teaspoon baking soda
1 cup buttermilk
2 cups plain flour
1 teaspoon cinnamon
1 teaspoon baking powder
½ teaspoon salt
1 cup prunes, cut up
½ cup prune juice
1 teaspoon vanilla

SAUCE
1 cup margarine
1½ cups brown sugar
1 cup condensed milk
1 box confectioners' sugar
1 teaspoon vanilla

Combine oil and sugar. Add eggs one at a time. Add soda to buttermilk. Sift dry ingredients together. Add flour mixture alternately with buttermilk. Fold in prunes and juice, add vanilla. Bake at 350°F for 30 to 35 minutes in a greased and floured broiler pan.

When cake has baked for 30 minutes, begin to prepare sauce. Cook first three sauce ingredients over low heat. Cool and add confectioners' sugar and vanilla. Pour sauce over cooled cake.

—BEATRICE NEWGARDEN

I don't understand why everybody's so mad at me. I was only trying to help. I figured a cookbook would help us raise some money, get us involved in a task together, create more love among the women at Hope Springs. But I just got off the phone with Louise, and she talked to me like I suggested we donate our kidneys, for goodness' sake. My mother always told me I was too good for that church, those women. I'm forever having to be the one to smooth things over, get people to talk to each other. And I just hope they realize that if I hadn't come in with this idea about the cookbook, our Women's Guild would not last another year.

The Good Lord knows that I have tried to breathe new life into that church by bringing in some younger women. But these girls today . . . they have aerobics classes and their careers in management. They have their children in everything there is imaginable. Why I even heard Rev. Stewart was planning to have some Chinese karate man using our fellowship hall to teach karate or kung fu or some Asian exercise that probably isn't Christian.

Things are just so complicated these days. Everybody's trying to do everything and getting nothing done. Nobody wants to pitch in and help at the church. I feel like it's all I can do to keep that little church up and running. Nobody has any sense of loyalty or responsibility anymore. And I don't see it any more clearly than I do in my own family. Robin has an important job at some bank in Charlotte. She'll probably never marry. Teddy keeps going to school for one thing and then another. And Jenny, bless her heart, the twins and that lazy husband of hers are all that she can handle.

In the beginning I tried to busy myself in their lives, be a real mother to them, but I was told in a hurry to mind my own business. And after Paul died I just assumed I could live with them throughout the year, especially during the winter, since the homeplace gets so cold. It's a daughter's duty, after all, to care for an aging mother. But that idea went nowhere.

Oh, I admit it hurt my feelings for a while, but I realized that they've got their own lives to lead. So I moved back home. And even though it took a while to adjust to living alone, I managed. I stayed busy with visiting the sick, taking cassette tapes of the Bible to the shut-ins, teaching crafts at the nursing home. I was home for about a year when Dick Witherspoon asked me if I would like to help over at the funeral home. Well, I never thought I would be one to do such a job, but it turns out to suit me very well.

I always did know how to put clothes together, and I've fixed hair since I was a little girl twirling strands of cotton. The makeup wasn't hard to learn. Pinks and rose mostly. Mr. Witherspoon says I'm the best funeral beautician he's ever seen. He says you would hardly know that those corpses are dead the way I fix them up. I like to think of it as my little ministry for the community and for those who suffer.

I know most of the dead. It's a small community after all. So I can usually remember how they flip their hair and how much lipstick they wear. I've got a good memory for how people look. And I am also very clear about what they could have done to look better. On occasion, it's this desire to better someone's appearance that has gotten me into trouble.

I almost got in a fight with Delores Wade over her mama. Delores claimed her mother had never had color in her hair and that I should leave the gray showing in the front. I knew perfectly well that Elsie Wade needed Clairol Number 83, natural black shade.

I had tried to tell Elsie while she was living in a loving, gentle way, like the Scriptures tell us to do, but you'd have thought I was telling her she needed a feminine hygiene spray. We were in the Wal-Mart at Burlington, standing at the shampoo aisle, just chatting, and I said, "Why, Elsie, I believe that if you tried this Clairol Number Eighty-three, you'd be very pleased with the results." She turned a funny shade of red, made a huffing kind of sound, and wheeled her buggy around so fast she knocked over the toothpaste display.

You know, thinking about that now, I remember that happened only a few weeks before she died. So that when they brought her into Witherspoon's, I figured here was my chance to lend Elsie some of the dignity she would never claim while she lived here on earth. But once again my good deed got punished.

Delores, the meddlesome daughter who moved up north after school, claimed her mama looked too young. The black hair wasn't natural. I said to her just as tenderly as I could, "Now, Delores, isn't that the point for women in life and in death?" I was only speaking the truth, but after I said it I was afraid the woman was going to hit me!

Dick, Mr. Witherspoon, said that even though he could see that I had done an excellent job with Elsie, the bereaved family needed to be pleased. Delores had apparently made things difficult for him. So I gave Elsie back that white chunk in the front and even streaked the back.

After that Mr. Witherspoon preferred that I let the family choose how to fix up their loved one. He agreed that I had a real eye for that sort of thing, but that in the funeral business, just like at Kmart, the customer is always right. So now I fix them up the way I remember they looked or the way they could have looked with a little help, take a picture, and then let the family tell me what they want to change. There's always something they want different, since I've learned there's nothing worse than a person in mourning having to make wardrobe decisions. I keep the picture as a sort of legacy to my work. Mr. Witherspoon said he used to do the same thing, but now he doesn't care to remember how many people he's buried.

I shouldn't complain about the families, since I know all about what grief can do to your memories. For the longest time after Paul died, I pretended we never had an argument. I'd have long conversations with the other women about how Paul never raised his voice and how we never let the sun go down on our anger. They would all smile and nod, pat me on my arm like I was so fortunate.

But in the more recent years, I've remembered things a little differently. Like how Paul never raised his voice because he rarely used it around me. And that we never had any arguments because we never talked. I realized that I had grown so accustomed to the silence that I began to invent reasons for it. Like he had too many things on his mind to speak about my new dress. Or he was all talked out from the last auction he called. I pretended over the years that we were comfortable and that the mediocrity that we both settled for was really happiness.

It never occurred to me that we didn't have anything to say to one another. That the silence was simply reflective of our marriage. Now don't hear me wrong; I'm not saying that Paul Newgarden was a bad husband or even that he was a bad man. He wasn't. He provided for his family. He bought the children toys on holidays, took us to the beach every summer, and even set me up my own savings account. He helped out around the house and did as much driving for the children as I did. He just didn't know how to love me. Not in the way I wanted.

There was always a gift for my birthday. Weekends there would be some little knick-knack he would pick up from an auction and bring home after the sale. He never missed taking me out to eat for our anniversary. All things that other women claim not to get from their husbands. But even these women, when they make this claim, make it with a depth of humor, some slapstick comment that makes me realize that there's some balance for what they do get that I'd never understand.

Like, for instance, maybe he doesn't bring her flowers but he can say her name in a way that reminds her of pure sweetness. Or maybe he forgets their anniversary but makes up for it by rubbing her feet and singing her some silly love song that makes her blush. So that even though a woman would complain about what her husband did or forgot to do, there would always be a lift to her voice when she remembered how he made it up to her.

Paul never forgot anything, leaving me with no grounds to complain and no memory of clever romance he used to win back my affections. He was sturdy and dependable, solid as Gibraltar, but the thing is that he never, not in the thirty-seven years that we were married, ever surprised me.

I've learned that some people like predictability, say that they need it. I know that I thought I did. But I wish Paul would have done at least one thing that I could remember with a smile and a shake of my head. Some story that I could think about and, even with twenty years having passed, still laugh at the thought, and know that it was so intimate that no one could understand.

Oh, I suppose I expected too much. Maybe I

read too many romance novels, but there was always something I needed that he could never give. Some part of him that was so closed off to himself that he did not have a clue as to how to open it to someone else, even, maybe especially, his wife.

And as soon as these thoughts came to me and I understood that the conversations that I was having at the graveyard were just as one-sided as they had always been, I quit going. I put the flowers out on significant holidays, but primarily I don't go out there. Jenny said something about it, asked why I didn't go anymore. I just shrugged like I didn't know. But the truth is, I figured I could find better things to do with my time, that I had wasted almost four decades talking to a dead man and I might as well not waste anymore.

I know that people whisper there's something going on between me and Dick at the funeral home. But it's all completely professional. He's never married, so there is certainly possibility for a relationship. But so far he's been a complete gentleman. Too much like Paul, in fact.

More than likely, I can tell you what he eats for lunch every day during the week and what jacket he'll wear to meet with which families. I've never been to his house, but I can pretty much guess that it's a tractor magazine that sits by his toilet and that he uses the same coffee cup every day. And I know enough to realize I don't need another arrangement of convenience, even if it would mean that the weekends wouldn't be so quiet. I think for now I'll enjoy the solitude and escape the disappointment of marriage.

Besides, I have enough to do, like this cookbook. Obviously, Louise isn't going to be much help, and Jessie has already said she doesn't have many recipes herself, so I told Margaret that I'd be more than happy to help her collect what she needs. I have a whole file of my own. Most people know that my mother was the best cook in Guilford County, and when I got old enough to write, I had her tell me everything she knew how to make. I have notebooks full. Now, of course, there are some recipes that I just won't share. It's silly, I know, since neither Robin nor Jenny will ever use them. But they were my mother's, and they're sacred to me, so that I don't want to throw all my pearls to the swine.

It wouldn't matter anyway. Church isn't what

it used to be. That little girl of a preacher tries, but I miss a man's voice in the pulpit. I love to hear the Psalms read by a rich bass voice. Her high-pitched tones put me to sleep. And, besides, she seems unsettled most of the time, like she's waiting for the other shoe to drop. Troubled, distracted in a way, like she's done something wrong. But as far as I know there have been no complaints about her. Even Dreama Isley hasn't said anything bad about her. That in itself is no small feat, since Dreama doesn't like anybody.

You know what I think would help? A hobby. If she had something to do that she really enjoyed, like flower arranging, maybe that would ease the edginess around her eyes. Young people without families need something to occupy their minds besides work. The young women especially. Surely she doesn't find any men to date, being in her position and all, she needs some leisure activity that can keep her busy and her mind off of her loneliness.

I think I'll hunt up a couple of my flower-arranging books, let her borrow them, and make her a prune cake. I've got all the recipes out anyway. I might as well try a couple, just to make sure they're right. And Lord knows, there's nothing like a good prune cake to smooth out the kinks.

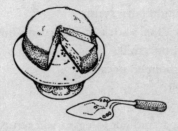

Jessie's Pecan Pie

———◈———

1 cup white sugar
Pinch of salt
3 beaten eggs
½ cup dark brown corn syrup
½ cup light corn syrup
Almost all of a stick of margarine, melted
1 teaspoon vanilla
1 cup chopped pecans
Pie shell

Add sugar and salt to eggs. Add syrup, margarine, and vanilla. Stir in pecans. Pour into pie shell. Bake at 300°F to 325°F for 45 to 50 minutes.

—JESSIE JENKINS

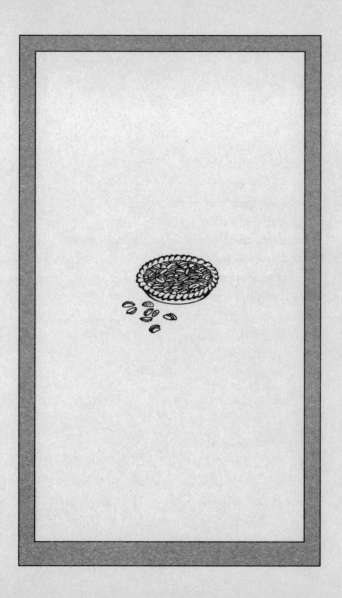

*N*ow surely those white women know that black women don't use recipes. We cook by what's in our heads, the tastes we remember in the backs of our mouths. The memories on the tips of our tongues. They're all the time wanting to know how much salt I put in the greens, how many eggs are in my pound cake. And when I tell them I can't remember, they holler, "Well look at the recipe card and call me."

I know they probably just think I'm being cantankerous or, worse, that I'm illiterate, but I don't have any recipe cards except what I got spinning around in my Rolodex brain. And I'm sure that if I did ever take the time to write down all that I know, I could fill up a book by myself. But black women never learn to cook from recipes.

Before my mama taught me to cook, she taught me to focus. So that when she started calling out the ingredients for whatever it was she was cooking, I was to call them back to her. "One cup of sugar," she'd say. And like a parrot, I'd repeat, "One cup of sugar." It was the way of learning back then. And even though we were calling out the spices in a pie or the number of teaspoons to dip from the canisters, it became like a prayer to us. A call and response like a song in the fields or a litany at Easter.

I grew up in a house full of women. Grandmothers, aunts, sister-in-laws, and mother. And they all could cook as well as they could tell a story. And those women could tell a story.

Unfortunately, we didn't have the luxury of writing things down. Not the stories and not the recipes. Most of the women I grew up around knew how to sign their names, and how to spell most words, but taking the time to put things to paper was too costly in matters of time and vision.

Grandmama taught me the alphabet when I was five, but she never learned how to put the letters together to spell a word. Mama was real smart, read the Bible through fifty-seven times, drew pictures, and quilted beautiful quilts. She could recite poetry and psalms, but she never wrote down a memory or a recipe. Maybe it was because she and the other women were never sure they would find what was needed for the recipe or because they knew that a person's memory on a page could never bring somebody else happiness.

Black women, in the early days, learned to cook by using whatever it was they happened to find growing in their backyards or whatever it was that the white women threw outside to rot. They never measured for taste. They spooned or folded or stirred whatever it was they had to spare. And if they didn't have sugar, they wrestled honey from bees. If they didn't have collards or turnips, they dug up poke leaves and dandelion roots.

Black women have always learned to improvise, and we never cooked directly for pleasure, only for survival. We never had the luxury to try something new or invent a dish for fun. Our women knew that if we messed up the stew, burnt the corn bread, or took too much skin off the bird, our family would go without a meal that day. So there wasn't any room for misreading the recipe card or not paying attention to what we were doing. We focused when we learned, and we were serious about how we cooked.

Don't get me wrong, though. I don't mean to say that mealtime wasn't joyful. In fact, it was the happiest time for our families. I suppose any time you're surviving, there's pleasure to be had. The men were pleased that they didn't have to watch their children go hungry, and the women were pleased because, just like Jesus, they had managed another food miracle for the family.

You ever notice how black women act when they hear that story about Jesus feeding the five thousand? They'll nod their heads and smile because they've seen it done. Every Friday in fact. Their man would come in with a couple of skinny little fish he had managed to catch with a worm and a string, and that woman would take those fish, batter them in leftover cornmeal, fry them up, squeeze a dozen biscuits from an inch of dough, make slaw from an old head of cabbage, and feed the whole neighborhood. Yeah, we know them Jesus stories like they were ours.

But you try to explain black women's cooking to white women and they look at you like you're speaking a different language. "No recipe? How can you cook this whole meal without a recipe?"

I just roll my eyes and walk away. There are some things that separate white women from black women. Cooking is only one of those things. The others have to do with emotional expression and how we like to sing in church. Black women are not afraid to wail from sorrow or holler out in joy. And when we worship, we expect to be just as moved by the choir as we are by the preacher. White women seem to value stillness and silence. Black women are going to make some noise.

I know it's strange that I'm going to an all-white church. I hear that it isn't so odd in the city, but out in the country, we're real clear about one another's places. It's like that caste system in India. You know where you're going to end up by the family into which you're born. It's clear and settled by the color of your skin. Like a sentence of life or death. And there ain't no amount of money, no amount of land or property going to change your destiny.

I remember crying about it when I was a little girl. Crying that I didn't have the pretty pink dresses that I had seen the little white girls wearing or crying that I couldn't go into the buildings and diners that they paraded into, and I wondered how things could be so separate for little girls. But Mama would rub my neck and wipe my face and say, "Jessie, that's just how it is. You ain't never going to have what those children have, but you've got to remember that what you do have is just as good and you are just as special."

Then she'd remind me of how I got to watch her make my dresses from her own or how I got to play with my brothers in the creek or in the tops of trees. That I was free to go into the black-owned businesses, the church, and everybody's houses that I loved. And before I knew it I was feeling good about my place, and I even found myself feeling a little sorry for the white girls, who couldn't run in their dress clothes or would never know the words to our jump rope songs. But feeling sad or feeling happy, I was always clear about our places. And even though over fifty years have passed, not much has changed in this part of the world.

I've seen white men spend more time working on a black folks' church than on their own
just to make sure that our places remain separate.
Oh, the women try to act like their menfolk are
doing the deed out of love, but I know better.
They're doing it to keep sticky black children
from dirtying up their velvet pews. They're doing it so they won't have to say out loud what
they know in their hearts. White people and
black people aren't supposed to sit side by side
and pray. White people and black people aren't
supposed to eat the same body and drink the
same blood.

In their minds it's real clear. And they can say
what they want about rebuilding and fixing up
the AME church down the road; they can go
ahead and say they're giving God the glory until
they're red in the face, but they aren't fooling
anyone, least of all the black folk.

I think I started going to Hope Springs on a
dare. It was about 1960. I was in my late twen-
ties, home from graduate school, radical and in-
spired. I didn't even believe in God anymore, but
I did believe in equal rights for everyone, equal
access, equal opportunities. I was sitting at the
table at my parents' home, spewing on about

how different things were going to be, how there were so many changes happening. And I think it was my older brother, Ervin, who said something like "If you're so sure things are moving so quickly, why don't you visit the church down the road? Why don't you hightail it right on up to that white church, sit on the front row, and just see how far those fancy speeches are going to get you in this community?"

So I did. Much to my family's surprise and fear, I went right by myself and sat on the first row. It was the most defiant thing I have ever done. And I was scared, looking all bad on the outside with my Afro and my beads, but inside I was afraid. Nervous as a cat.

Funny thing was that it turned out that the pastor was a decent man. He was probably in his seventies, had been there more than twenty years, and had a lot of respect from the congregation. So that when he visited me at my parents' home, asked me to teach youth Sunday School, and went with me to my grandmother's funeral, the white church people paid attention and carried on likewise.

I never heard a harsh thing from or about the man. And, better, I never experienced anything

ugly or spiteful from the membership. Now I'm
quite sure that behind the doors there was
plenty of talk, but in my presence I never experienced anything but loving-kindness. His
goodness rubbed off on them, made them a better people. And I believe that's the greatest thing
to say about a minister.

He wasn't a very good preacher. The services
were lifeless, and his sermons were dry. But after
the reasons of protest wore off and I was forced
to look again at why I went there, I discovered I
needed to hear the way he talked to God. His
prayers walked me back to faith, and, praise the
Lord, I've never turned away.

That's been more than thirty years ago now. I
got married in that church, baptized my babies
in that church, even buried my parents in the
side cemetery, something the funeral director in
the black community said would never happen.
I know that it's been a stretch for most of those
folks to have me there, but I've found my place.
I belong. So I stay.

We've probably been through nine or ten
preachers since then. Some good. Some not so
good. But we've managed to stay together and,
for the most part, not let issues of race cloud our

worship. The Wilmington Ten incident cost us some members, was hard on everybody, but, like good friends, we managed through. I'd say it's been a blessing, for all of us. It has not, of course, been without its struggles, but, then again, most real blessings require some wrestling.

Rev. Stewart is the first woman preacher we've had. She's young, same age as my Janice, inexperienced, grew up just a few miles up the road. We can't pay her much, but we have a nice parsonage and we keep her fed. She worries a lot, and I expect has more mothers than she needs, but we're pushing along. She seems glad to have me there. Like my presence somehow eases her liberal tendencies. Like I'm the balance for everything else bigoted and unjust in the community. She can say to her peers that Hope Springs isn't all-white, and that because of my family she can claim to have an integrated congregation. I think I help ease some of her white guilt. I know that I've done that for more than one minister here.

Most of my children are close by. Everyone except Annie. She moved up to Washington with her husband. She gets homesick a lot, but I've told her what my mother told me: "When you marry, you go with your husband. His people become your people. Give it five years, and if it still doesn't work, you can come home."

James Junior lives next door. He works nights and tries to make a go of it farming. He's a good son, married to a girl he met in high school. She takes him and the family over to the Baptist church near Burlington, where she grew up.

Robert is in Greensboro; he teaches school and has never married. And Janice, having lived out the five-year contract, moved home, changed her name back to ours, and lives at home with me and her son, Wallace. She changed his name too. He's sixteen and acts older than his mother. He's also the only one who will go to church with me.

James Senior, who claims he married me for my pies, left home when the girls started high school. He made it sound like it was finishing up military duty or schooling, talking about how he had "put in his time" and that now he was going to enjoy life. Guess a pie isn't enough to hold a marriage together. I think I probably knew that he was leaving by the time our second child was born, but I kept hoping.

That's one thing I learned isn't different between white women and black. We are always hoping. Hoping it won't rain on our washing. Hoping our children will get home safe from school. Hoping the lump in our breast is just dried-up milk, and hoping our husbands will love us when we're old. That last hope for me withered up and blew away more than fifteen years ago. That's when James Senior left.

We've yet to get officially divorced, and from time to time I hear from him. A postcard, a phone call. He sends a check regularly. The children know he loves them. But he's never come home, and I've never asked him to. I managed a good living keeping the books at the mill in town. I've always been good with numbers. "A gift," my mama would say. So I worked my way up from the weaving line to the front office and from angry protester to union president.

With or without a husband, I've done better than most of the women in my family. And even though the nights are long and lonely, I'd rather be without him than worrying that he's going to leave me. At least I don't have that unsettled sense about me like the other women my age whose husbands keep coming home a little later every night with that distant look in their eyes.

At least I know where I stand, and I stand there just fine. At least I have that. And I don't have to wonder anymore whether or not this time he won't come back. Like somebody who's been figuring on getting cancer all their life and finally hears the diagnosis, at least I know. I do have that. But there's nothing more, and sometimes I feel as cold as a stone inside. Cold as a stone.

Unfortunately, I do still think of him every time I bake a pie. When I'm pressing down the edges with my thumbs, it all comes back. Like calling on the old memory of how to cook a meal, I wander into the forgotten places of desperation. Hope. Thinking with the heart of a woman, that maybe, just maybe, this one will do the trick.

It's a mindless journey, I know. But still I go. And because I let myself wander this way, pie recipes turn out to be the only recipes I will write down.

Charlotte's Banana Pudding

———◦◦◦———

1 tablespoon flour
¾ cup sugar
1 ½ cups scalded milk
1 egg, beaten
1 teaspoon vanilla
⅓ stick margarine
3 to 4 ripe bananas
Vanilla wafers

Combine flour and sugar. Add to scalded milk and cook over low heat. Add some hot mixture to egg, then add to mixture. Cook over low heat until thick. Stir constantly so mixture does not lump. Stir in vanilla and margarine. Layer with bananas, sliced, and wafers. Crumble vanilla wafers for topping.

—REVEREND CHARLOTTE STEWART

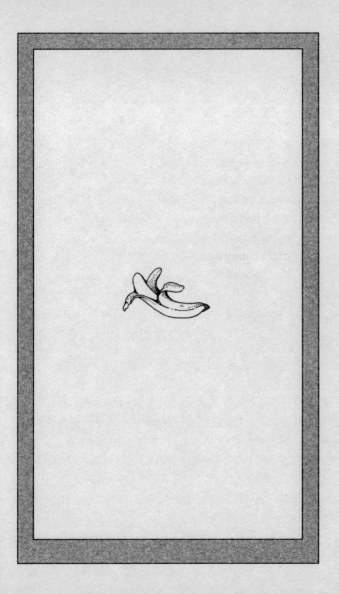

I know as much about cooking as I do about trying to explain the doctrine of the Trinity to a four-year-old. What was Nadine Klenner thinking when she told little Brittany that I could explain it to her? I'll tell you what she was thinking: "That preacher doesn't have anything to do this afternoon, here's my babysitter while I go get my nails done!" That's exactly what she was thinking.

A couple of months ago she claimed Brittany wanted to know all about baptism. I planned out some Bible verses to read to her, got her a little coloring book called "Dancing in the Water," and even filled up the font to give her a demonstration. When Nadine dropped her off, Brittany went straight to the nursery, where she stayed for the entire hour while her mother did their grocery shopping. She had no interest in going to the sanctuary, seeing the baptism font, or coloring pictures of a baby being sprinkled. She wanted to play house in the refrigerator box that the nursery teacher had brought to church the Sunday before.

This time she's probably set on testing out the little Wurlitzer organ somebody donated. I suppose I should tell Nadine that she has to stay with us, eliminate this baby-sitting pattern, besides I don't know any male preacher who would baby-sit a four-year-old, but Nadine has a way of getting what she wants with me. She reminds me of my sister. An empty glass trying to fill herself up. Always managing to find somebody who'll drain themselves dry in order to give her an ounce of living. I poured myself out a long time ago, so I should know how to put the top on with Nadine. But somehow I feel myself open up like a carton of milk when she walks into the room.

Serena never meant harm. It was the way she coped. The way she managed the life that was handed to us. For as long as I can remember she was living off me. My paycheck, as small as it was, my friends, my homework, my fears and my faith. I had only a few resources in knowing how to deal with our mother, Joyce. Serena had none except for the ones she borrowed from me. Thinking about it now, maybe that was more or better than having her own.

I could tell when Joyce fell off the wagon just by the distance Serena let between herself and me. Somehow it would be she that would awake to the late-night binges first, and it wouldn't be long before I would feel her hot, sticky breath next to my face. I'd slide over, and she'd crawl in the bed next to me.

Even now, as time progresses, I find that my body remembers her in the way my mind forgot. Like at night, when the darkness is as thick as wool, the moon clouded over, and the streetlight is hidden in the tree limbs, I still feel her spooned around my back, her arm carelessly thrown about my shoulder. She is still in me. Drained as I feel of most emotion, I still carry my sister deep inside my heart.

Hope Springs was a surprise. They called me right after seminary graduation. Their pastor left them after only a few months. "Got a bigger church," they said. Mrs. Peele was the chair of the search committee. She heard me preach at a women's day service at the church on campus. She knew I was from the area, so she asked me to preach during the summer until they found an interim minister.

That was eighteen months ago. I moved from supply preaching to becoming the interim pastor to six months later being permanent. It seemed like a natural progression, just like the passing of school year to school year. And though we haven't ever really discussed it, I think most everybody is satisfied.

Because, as best as I can tell, things are going okay. However, I'll be honest, and it's hard for me to admit, but I realize now that I haven't always been prepared. Not for the big stuff and certainly not for the little stuff. And sometimes in church, I've learned, the little stuff is the big stuff. Part of my job, I'm discovering, is that I'm supposed to know the difference. And sometimes I don't. I just don't.

Like printing the bulletin. I think the order of service and the announcements should flow, be like a hymn or a litany of praise, but all I get are complaints that I put the middle son's name before the first daughter's on the flower memorials. Or that the inserts are too long. I've learned that most of the folks don't read them anyway. They don't seem to have much appreciation for any written material other than *The Farmer's Almanac.*

There are times when I'm just not sure that I'm cut out for this preaching business. Looking back, I think maybe Daddy was right; I should have been a nurse or a teacher. At least that way you're able to see your patients get better or your students graduate. You have some sense that you're making a difference, that your project is complete. In the church you can never tell if anyone's getting any better or if anybody's learned a thing. It's like a long, dry summer, the only success you can claim is in naming what hasn't died.

Everybody's always asking about why I wanted to be a preacher. It's a natural curiosity, I suppose. I never knew any women ministers. And though I wish I had some brilliant story of a mountaintop calling, some bush burning on a hill calling out my name, I know that my story isn't nearly so extravagant. I received a full scholarship to divinity school because of the urging of a religion professor. Since no one else took the time to nominate me for any other graduate school scholarships and I truly admired Dr. Little, I went ahead to seminary and finished the course of study in the recommended three years.

I started going to the Methodist church when I was little. A neighbor took Serena and me in an attempt to make things better for us. Joyce called it meddlesome, but I would still go every Sunday because I loved church. I loved the order of it all. Families sitting together. Mothers and fathers and squirming children, all bunched in tidy rows. A bulletin that spelled out exactly what would happen from beginning to end. Hymnbooks and Bibles with everybody on the same page. Everyone had the understanding that rarely would there be a surprise in church. And I, the daughter of an alcoholic, I longed for an hour without surprises. An hour of cleanliness, order, and clearly defined boundaries. So that church became that solid rock in my sea of disarray. It was where I went to quiet the chaos.

I never had what I would call a religious experience in church. There was never too much emotionalism. And the preacher only came to our house once. As most people did. I joined the church when I was twelve and went regularly right up until college. In all my years of perfect attendance in Sunday School, Vacation Bible School, summer camp, and revival there was never really anything unusual. I never witnessed one miracle, unless you count the tree face.

It was Jimmy Rudgers who showed me the countenance of Christ that had just appeared on the surface of the remains of the old tree at the back of his grandmother's tobacco barn. It was mesmerizing and strange. A miracle, to be sure. Jesus' face set and peeling into the center of a rotten tree trunk. Long hair and eyes set off in the distance, a crown of thorns around his head. He was not quite the clean and smooth-skinned man I had envisioned, but it was still him peering at us from the table of a tree. And we dared not tell anyone for fear the gift would vanish.

Every Saturday morning for a month we would meet at the shrine. I never spoke of where I was going, not even to Serena. Jimmy and I would light matches around the secret sanctuary and pray for stuff to happen: my mother to quit drinking, and his older brother to suffer the consequences of meanness. All week I waited for the chance to visit the wooden Christ. I collected flowers, beads from my jewelry. I even stole a dollar from Joyce's purse to leave at the altar that was mine only to share with Jimmy Rudgers.

In defiance of our pact of always going together, I went to the face alone on a Tuesday when I cut my lip on the water fountain. Butch Rierdon snuck up behind me when I was getting a drink and forced my head into the spout. My bottom lip was split, and I was sent home. Since Joyce was never known to show up in times of emergency, I walked home by way of the stump. In the daze of that warm autumn day, I knelt before the face of Christ, touched my swollen, torn lip to his, and felt the skin grow back together.

I never even told Jimmy. So that when he finally confessed that he and his brother had made the carving the summer before, that it was no miracle after all, I was not even angry at their practical joke. I only smiled, licking the line on my lip that had become the only evidence I had that I was special.

Since then, the scar has practically disappeared, and my life as a spiritual person is more of an intellectual journey than an emotional or even a faithful one. I moved from class to class, level to level, concentrating on the tasks given, the expectations of professors and committees, and jumping through the hoops placed before me. I was the perfect student, who has always played by the rules without ever asking for anything special. Even when Serena died, I did not pause.

The president of the school called after the chaplain had heard the news and contacted him. He arranged a sort of medical leave for me. But I only missed four days of classes. One to identify the body, since Joyce was too drunk and Daddy was out of town. Two for the visitation and funeral. And one to clean out her things from my mother's apartment. I left Joyce passed out on the kitchen floor, drove back to seminary, and took my exams.

I don't think of myself as wounded or dysfunctional because of my upbringing or lack of family ties. I can't believe that my life is so terrible. I appreciate that I'm rarely surprised. I have low expectations of what life has to offer. And I like being in control. Frankly, it's much more satisfying than being out of control. Or so it appears. I don't know of a time when I wasn't in control. Even sitting before the face of Jesus, I never permitted myself too much imagination. I was always very sure of where and who I was. There are some things even Jesus can't change.

When I got the job as pastor of Hope Springs, I didn't tell Joyce. She found out in November of that first year. Even though she swore she had been sober six months, I was still too worried that she'd show up one Sunday morning hungover or drunk. I managed to keep her out of it until she ran across my name in the paper in the wedding section. I believe I had just married Penny Throckmorton and that sailor the Friday before. Anyway, Joyce came in the next Sunday. And she was, I'm happy to say, on her best behavior.

Oh, the women were so happy to meet her. They treated her like a queen for the day. She was cordial, polite, even proud. But afterwards I asked her not to come back. Now when folks ask me where she is, I tell them she's Episcopalian and goes over to the church in downtown Greensboro. So far, I've not been bothered by her or the church people wanting her back.

Daddy comes to town every couple of years. That's about as much as he gets back to North Carolina. He's been in Texas for seventeen years.

When he left Joyce he married again right away. That one didn't last either. But now he's married to Judy VanBerken, and I think because her family's got a little money he's going to try and stick it out. We've not talked much since I went to college, and I've never told him that I admire him for his willingness to keep looking for happiness. Unlike me, he always seemed to know there was something better than what he had. He's never quit believing that it might just come to him as long as he stays interested.

I suppose I would look too if I believed that there is something better out there for me, but, for the most part, I'm satisfied with my life. I don't want for much anymore. And the most I look for is to keep from being surprised, caught off guard, or running into the unexpected.

There are, of course, some aspects of being a pastor that I hate. The late hours. The pettiness of some of the membership. The endless committee meetings. Sometimes it feels more like running a business than the house of God.

But there are also some things that I love. Like being able to bless stuff. Marriages, babies, families. I even blessed Myrtle Simpleton's back porch because she was afraid a demon had camped out there. It is such a feeling of power to summon forth the forces of the universe, the nodding of God at the beckoning of my voice, the touch of my hand. And in the moment when I bring the blessing down upon the person or relationship or object of one's fear, even though I feel nothing, I like to think I am a lightning rod, a vehicle of grace. The power alive and surging through me. It never matters where or when or with whom, I still like the thought of calling on the name of God.

The rest of the time, though, I simply try to maintain the order. Keep programs for all the age groups, Bible studies, visitation, fellowship. It's a lot of work to manage the faith and entertainment of a congregation, and I'm always trying to keep everyone comfortable. I guess that sense of trying to create balance is starting to show. Everybody seems concerned that I work too much and that I appear tired all the time or that I have no hobby or leisure activity. Mrs. Newgarden even brought me books on flower arranging the other day. Could it be that I appear so unhealthy that I need a book on flower arranging?

And, only recently, one older minister down the road, the Lutheran, who was out weeding in his garden on a Tuesday morning, told me I needed to "cool my jets" and understand that for the most part the preaching business is to "hatch, match, and dispatch," so that there was no reason to burn myself out trying to do anything other than baptisms, weddings, and funerals.

I was surprised at his advice. I know that I looked shocked, disappointed. But I realized that, of course, there is an element of truth to what the old guy said. There is a need for balance. And yet I still keep pushing, wanting to believe that I am capable of doing a little something more for this church, though I don't know what that is. Still, I'm not naive. I know that the church is not growing. I see the heads get grayer and grayer, the nursery and children's Sunday School get smaller and smaller. I understand that the reason they hired me was because they didn't want to pay what a man requires and that they just don't want to close the church doors while they're alive.

I see the apathy, the clutching to traditions, and I recognize that the circles I'm running in don't add up to much of anything for these folks. Both Mrs. Peele and Mrs. Jenkins have told me to slow down, take it easy, and I trust them more than anyone else in the church, but somehow deep inside me I know that I'm afraid that if I stop or even slow down, this flame I've decided is faith will burn out for everyone. Perhaps or especially for me.

And in the midst of fanning flames, I try to make myself believe that maybe there is a God somewhere orchestrating this entire arrangement, and that maybe time will bring healing and I might come to appreciate what I don't plan. I like the notion that seasons can pass, that Sunday can run to Sunday, and that God is capable of moving today like he did in the Old Testament with the children of Israel.

I like to imagine that God is a cloud rolling over our sorrows and our disappointments. Picking up that which is unbearable and pulling it into his great growing mass. A pillar of fire warming our dreams and the desires of our hearts. I like to think of God as small flakes of heaven's bread falling like snow all around us. Tiny pieces of sugar, unrecognizable joy, that land in our hair, on the lids of our eyes, and on the wounded and seeping places in our hearts.

I like to think that there is reason and purpose to all the pain and all the emptiness we do not understand, that God is making a way for all of his children to be led into some promised land. And, like driving through an ice storm, a long ways from home, someday we will see the light on the porch and know where we are, even appreciate where we've been. A home where everything is finally all right with a welcome that surpasses any I've ever had.

This is what I like to think when I sit at my desk writing a sermon or planning a prayer, but mostly I am just keeping my eyes on a long and winding, barren road. Driving ahead like some undeterred soldier, looking neither left nor right. Eyes only forward, hoping that I might see the cloud, the fire, a little speck of snow, and maybe the light on the porch. And, even though I know it's hopeless, really, it's all I've got.

So I drive on. Straight then curve then stop then straight. It is a cadence of survival that keeps me in motion. I baby-sit. I preach. I write recipes. Speaking of which, maybe I can find the banana pudding recipe that Joyce's mother used to make and bring us. That should work for this Women's Cookbook. If Brittany is not interested in the Father, Son, and Holy Ghost, perhaps I'll have time to find it and jot it down.

Relishes
and
Pickles

Rose Mary's Squash Pickles

8 cups sliced squash
2 cups sliced onions
½ cup sliced green bell peppers
1 tablespoon salt
1 cup vinegar
½ teaspoon celery seed
½ teaspoon mustard seed
1¾ cups sugar

Combine squash, onions, and peppers.
Sprinkle with salt. Set aside for about 1
hour. Combine vinegar, seeds, and sugar,
and bring to a hard boil. Add the other
ingredients and bring to a boil again. Then
put in jars and seal.

—ROSE MARY JONES

"As the president of the Women's Guild, I'd like to call this meeting to order." Beatrice was sitting in the front of the Women's Bible Classroom behind the teacher's desk. "We all know that Rev. Stewart is at the hospital with Rose Mary. Did anybody make out from the scanner exactly what happened to J.T.?"

The classroom was neatly arranged in four rows of six chairs. The cement walls had been painted green, with various pictures of Jesus hanging on the front wall and on the sides. The window in the back was opened because the evening was warm and the room was stuffy. It was late in the summer, with an air that was stiff and heavy. The women looked around at each other, unwilling to claim that the story they had already repeated five or six times was the real story.

"The way I understood it, they gave him a couple of nitroglycerin tablets and put the oxygen mask on him before they drove him to the hospital. I suspect it was his heart." Elizabeth Garner's son was on the Rescue Squad, so she generally had the final word about the tragedies in the community. Beatrice shook her head in a sympathetic manner and shifted in her seat.

"Well, knowing that Rose Mary is needing our thoughts and concern, Jessie, would you open us with prayer?"

Now, if the truth be told about the Hope Springs Community Church Women's Guild, most of the women would admit that they were not comfortable with Jessie praying. No one ever said anything about it, not because they were worried about being called racist, that thought never crossed their minds as a thing about which to worry. They didn't speak about this mostly because they were less comfortable with having to pray themselves. And knowing that Margaret could get wind of their complaints and speak the truth—namely that if they didn't like Jessie's praying then why don't they

open up the meetings with their more appropriate prayers?—they kept their anxious thoughts
to themselves.

They were unsettled with Jessie's praying because they all thought that she prayed a little too
desperately, a little too burdened. It made them
feel like something was going to happen that
they weren't sure they were ready for. She had a
hunger, a gnawing in her prayers that seemed to
magnify the emptiness in their own spirits. And,
frankly, that troubled them. They braced themselves every time she bowed, and even though
most of them had been with Jessie for more
than twenty years and were used to her plead-
ings with God, her voice, her words, and the way
she shook her head still made them squirm.

Jessie stood and prayed. "O Holy Maker of
Heaven and Earth, we beseech you to enter into
our hearts and hear the cries of our souls. We
acknowledge that you are slow to anger and
quick with mercy, so forgive us our trespasses as
we look to find ways to forgive those who tres-
pass against us. We pray, O Holy One, that you
are with our dear sister Rose Mary. May the
goodness of your heavenly being comfort and
abide with her sorrowing and anxious heart. We

know, O God of Love, that you alone can heal us, so we pray that you place your hand upon our brother J.T.'s torn and battered body; and, if it be your will, make his heart and mind whole and bring him home to his loving wife and family. Our spirits are heavy with concern for our dear sister and brother. Take now this worry from our hearts and create glory for yourself in the healing of this one. And now may the grace of the Lord Jesus cleanse us from every sin and enable us to order our business at hand in the fashion of his words and deeds. In the name of the Father and of the Son and of the Holy Ghost. Amen." She sat down in silence while the room swayed back into place.

"Thank you, Jessie." Beatrice stood up from the table and read from the New Testament from the Book of James and then requested the treasurer's report, which was read by Twila Marks and approved by the body of the Guild. Margaret read the minutes from the last meeting with no changes made.

Beatrice continued, "Moving on to old business. I sent the check to the Methodist church for their migrant missions project, and I sent four get-well cards to those who were mentioned in our last meeting. Is there anything that I missed?"

No one spoke up. She went on. "Then, still in line with old business, what's the latest on the cookbook, Madam Secretary?"

Margaret blew a puff of air through her lips. "Well, Madam President"—she said this with a certain amount of flavor—"the latest is that I've got one recipe from all the members of the committee, one from the preacher, and Rose Mary's squash pickle card that she sent before she went to the hospital. Let's see, that makes eight. And I guess I don't have to tell you, eight recipes doesn't a cookbook make."

Louise rolled her eyes and crossed her arms heavily about her chest. It was a gesture that everyone noticed. A breeze stirred from the window.

Beatrice paused, unsure that she really should say anything, unclear of where this was heading. "You look like you're wanting to add something, Louise"; then she braced herself for the worst.

Louise was surprised at the opportunity to speak. She shook her head, then began. "I think you know my feelings about this little project, but being one who's not afraid to state the obvious, Beatrice, look around you. There's eleven women who come to these meetings. Eleven! And that's when we're all here. As much as I know you want us to do something, a cookbook is just not the best idea."

The other women looked around nervously. Louise always pushed the envelope beyond the limits of Southern politeness. In their minds, she went too far, and tonight, even though they agreed with her, they all thought she spoke a little too quickly.

After a long and stunned silence, Jessie stood up. "Beatrice, I have to agree with Louise. We just don't have what it takes to put a book together. It was a good idea, but only if we were a larger group. We just can't do this by ourselves." She sat down.

There was a long pause; another quick breeze poured into the room, and Twila got up to shut the window.

"So that's it then?" Beatrice looked like an old party balloon. Tired and flat. In fact, the women were sure that she was going to cry.

Nothing. Only the squeak and pull of a window trying to be brought down. The women looked at their feet, into their hands, at the pictures of Jesus, but no one looked at Beatrice.

"There is no other opinion?" The Women's Guild was silent. Thick with possibility but only silent.

"Well, since you're all agreed, I guess there's no need for a vote. And since I don't know of any new business, the meeting's adjourned." Beatrice got up from the table, packed up her Bible and her devotional calendar, and headed towards the door. She was steady and unsteady all at the same moment. She turned back to face the surprised gathering of church women and with a thready voice said, "Oh, and one more thing, I quit." She turned and placed her hand on the doorknob.

More than one gasp went up from the ladies. They had never seen Beatrice Newgarden be so defeated. They had never had a confrontation. They had never ended a meeting without refreshments!

"Wait just a damn minute, Beatrice." It was Louise. "This isn't a personal vendetta against you. We just don't like the idea is all. Can't you be president without having to have your way all the time?"

The women twitched and pulled at their dresses, at their hair. This was much too controversial for a meeting at the church.

Twila was still trying to close the window, though no one seemed to notice. "Could somebody please help me?"

Louise turned to the back of the room. "Good God, Twila, if you can't pull the window down, just leave the damn thing open."

Twila, being a polite and gracious lady, was completely caught off guard at such an attack from Louise. She could never remember actually having someone curse at her, and especially not at a Christian women's meeting. Her bottom lip began to tremble, but she kept her back to the group.

Finally it was Margaret who spoke. "Louise Fisher, what is your problem? You haven't done a thing since the first mention of this cookbook but bite people's heads off. Maybe you should have stayed at home tonight."

Louise looked at Margaret, then back at the wounded Twila, who was still trying with a very feeble attempt to push the window down.

"I'm sorry," Louise mumbled. "Twila," she shouted, "I said I'm sorry." She got up and helped her close the window. Twila looked at her and nodded without standing too close.

"And now, Beatrice, come back here and sit down." Margaret had moved to the front of the room. "You are not going to resign as president. You are going to hear our complaints about this cookbook project. And you are going to make suggestions about how we can get more recipes."

Both Beatrice and Louise snapped their heads around to look at Margaret.

"Yes, we will do the cookbook." She turned to square off with Louise. "And I suggest that if you've got anything to say about it, you say it now and you say it to me."

Louise knew when she was whipped. And she was always whipped by Margaret. With resignation, she said, "Fine."

Jessie gave a laugh while Beatrice moved back to the front desk. Without taking a breath she began. "I think that if we write a letter to all the families in the church asking for their favorite recipe . . ."

Earnestine Williams interrupted. "You could ask other churches in the community. I expect the Lutherans and the women over at Union

Grove Methodist could give us some recipes. Millie Townsley is a good cook from over there."

Dorothy West and Lucy Jackson nodded in agreement.

"Yes, but if we invite the other churches to participate, it's no longer our cookbook, it's the whole area's cookbook. What would that do to our title?"

"Title?" Louise asked as she went back to her seat. "You already have a title?"

"Well, nothing too elaborate or anything, just the Hope Springs Community Church Women's Guild Cookbook."

"Oh, that's catchy," Louise snapped.

"Beatrice, I have to go with Louise on this one, that's a little too wordy." Margaret had moved back to her seat as well.

"The point is not the title, the point is whether or not we want to ask for help from outside the church." Jessie was always able to get right to the point. "And I suppose that if we ask for assistance from the other churches, then we've got to be ready to pay them a part of what we take in."

"Is this about money? I didn't think this had

anything to do with money." Sarah Clayton was the one to ask the question.

"Goodness no," exclaimed Beatrice. "After we get through with the printing and the paper costs, there probably won't be any money."

"Then, refresh my memory, Beatrice, exactly why are we putting this book together?" Louise looked over to Margaret and shrugged her shoulders as if the question was innocent.

"Well, it's because . . ." Beatrice stammered a bit. She had not considered, in her preparations for the women's meeting, the possibility that she would have to share this aspect of the project, which, truth be told, she did not firmly grasp. She had made no notes on such as this. "It's so that, um, it's because we need to come together as a group and do something together, you know, as a group."

"Uh-huh." Louise shook her head. All of this was so beyond her.

"Oh, all right, Miss Louise Fisher." Beatrice planted herself. She saw no reason to hold back anything else. It was the free-for-all that Louise seemed to invite and that Beatrice was now ready to join. "I thought this cookbook was a good way for us to work together, maybe spend some quality time together."

Louise shifted in her seat and sighed, but Beatrice would not be turned away. She was not comfortable with the depth of the discussion, but she kept pushing herself deeper and further into the reasoning for the cookbook. Her face flushed and tight, she kept spilling out.

"I thought we needed something to . . ." Beatrice searched for the words. She was trying to explain in just the right way. Then she stopped and calmed herself.

"I thought maybe this might be the chance for us to become . . ." The corners of her mouth loosened. Her chin fell. Her shoulders rounded, and she took a breath. She dropped her head and studied the top of the desk, then lifted her face and spoke to the back of the room, the recently closed window, the pale green walls, and the women she had known for most of her life. ". . . for us to become friends."

All of the women looked at Beatrice and then looked away. In that split second of soft-ness, they fell back to a time of years gone by when they blushed more easily, laughed a little more quickly, and were surprised by tenderness.

A wash of days when they loved their secrets and loved telling them even more. A time lost and forgotten when nothing was more important than sharing a dream with someone who knew everything about them. It was true and silly and sad. They had outgrown the awkward and simple ways girls become friends.

"My Lord, Bea." Jessie had her chin in her left hand, and that was all she would say for a few silent minutes while the women hurried their spirits back to the things at hand. "I think you have a very noble idea." She sat up tall in her seat. "I make the motion that we keep the cookbook in our fellowship and use the opportunity to collect recipes as a chance"—she smiled in the direction of Louise—"to learn each other a little better."

Margaret nodded in triumph and touched the arm of Jessie, who was sitting next to her. "I second that motion."

Beatrice was embarrassed. She had opened up the lid on her heart and now fumbled to tighten it back on. She replied quietly, "We have a motion and a second, any discussion?" There was a long and steady pause as everyone turned towards Louise. "Then all in favor say Aye."

"Madam Secretary, please note that the Women's Guild has voted unanimously to collect recipes from the members of Hope Springs for our upcoming cookbook."

"So noted," said Margaret, writing the words down in her secretary's notebook. "Now, why don't we adjourn for refreshments?" She closed the book and winked at Beatrice.

"I think that's a great idea," remarked Twila, and she hurried out the door to the kitchen to begin preparations.

"We haven't had our program yet." Beatrice shuffled through her papers. "But I guess we don't have to do that tonight. After all, maybe some of us should go to the hospital to be with Rose Mary. Okay, then, the meeting is adjourned. Earnestine, will you lead us in a blessing for our food?"

Earnestine spun around to Jessie like she needed help and then led everyone in the Lord's Prayer.

Walking towards the kitchen, Margaret came up beside Louise. She was going to give her the chance to let her have it. It was Margaret's way to make amends, give Louise a clean and easy shot.

"Roxie has Alzheimer's." It was so blunt and quick Margaret wasn't even sure she remembered who Roxie was. They walked through the hallway past the nursery until they came into the kitchen and stood together in front of the table where the refreshments had been displayed. Most of the other women were ahead of them.

"Twila just said that Sylvia Hilton had a lot of recipes from her mother's diner over in Liberty, Fran's Front Porch. Maybe we could borrow some from her. You know how folks love that place." Beatrice came over and had returned to herself. She was filled with new air.

"That's a very good idea, Bea." Margaret turned to Louise, who poured herself a cup of coffee and walked around the table to stand next to Jessie, who was arranging cookies on a plate.

"Thank you for handling Louise for me." Beatrice nodded with her chin over towards Louise. She sidled next to Margaret like they were somehow closer than before the evening began.

"I'm not quite comfortable with the notion that I handled anyone, Bea. And even though she can sometimes be a little obstinate, Louise did speak out loud what most of those women were thinking. She's really not the enemy." Margaret looked over at Louise, wondering about the announcement she had made about Roxie. Had she wanted some response? Margaret thought.

Just as she was about to go over and ask for more details, Rev. Stewart walked in the door. All the women turned and looked at her. They were waiting for the report on J.T. and Rose Mary.

"You all are eating a little early tonight, aren't you?" Charlotte smiled, and Beatrice was quick to answer.

"We finished our business and decided to go ahead and have the refreshments. Have you had supper? Please, help yourself to something. And tell us what is happening at the hospital."

Rev. Stewart looked tired. They were used to that. So her physical appearance did nothing to cause them to think in one way or another about J.T.'s survival. She was wearing a pale blue dress that was much too long. There was a stain just below the neckline.

"He's okay. They were able to stabilize him and run some tests. He'll have to have surgery, but they're going to wait until he's not in so much pain. Are those chocolate chip?"

Sarah nodded. She was proud that her cookies had been mentioned. "Sure. The ones on the top have nuts."

"That's really good news about J.T. Is Rose Mary at the hospital alone?" Jessie had walked closer to the table where everyone else was standing.

"No, the children had come in by the time I left. After the doctor came and gave them the report, they were all going down to the cafeteria for some supper. So, how was your meeting?"

"Great," replied Beatrice, not giving anyone else the chance to speak first. "We're going ahead with the cookbook, and things are just great."

Louise cleared her throat and drank down the last of her coffee. "Well, ladies, I've caused enough damage for one evening, I'm going to head home. Earnestine, would you like to ride with me?"

Earnestine looked around, surprised at her neighbor's sudden announcement. "Um, sure, let me just get my cake plate."

"Okay, so, good night, everyone." Louise threw away her trash and walked back towards the meeting room to get her purse and Bible.

"Good night, Louise." It was Twila trying to convince herself and the others that there were no hard feelings.

Louise nodded in her direction.

"I'll call you later," Margaret said. But Louise had already left the kitchen.

The women glanced around at each other and then looked away quickly.

"Wow, it is later than I thought." Jessie was studying her watch. All the other women then looked at theirs as well. With sunlight lasting way into the evening hours, it was always a surprise to discover that the day was gone. It was 8:45.

Small talk continued well past 9:15. Twila and Lucy cleaned up the table while Beatrice made a little plate for the preacher to take home with her. Margaret and Jessie walked out together, the other women close behind them, and Beatrice and Charlotte were the last ones in the church.

"So, your meeting went well, I hope." Charlotte walked to the sink to put her glass down.

"It was a bit rocky at the beginning, but we hung in there and were able to carry out the important business." Beatrice was wiping the seats of the chairs.

"Hmm." Charlotte said this out loud, wondering how the word *rocky* might be thought of in referring to a Women's Guild meeting. It seemed quite incompatible.

Beatrice sat down on one of the chairs she was cleaning. "You know, when it's quiet in here, I feel like I hear angels humming."

Charlotte was tying up the trash bag and putting the top on the can. "I think it's just the refrigerator, Mrs. Newgarden, but that's a nice sentiment."

"No, it's deeper than that. Beneath the buzz of the icebox. It's like a current running through the place, something alive and old."

Charlotte stopped and listened. She turned her head first one way and then the other. She could hear the drag and pull of the electrical appliances, the swishing sounds of a car going past, a distant chirp of crickets, but she could hear no heavenly hum.

Then she looked at Beatrice. Her head leaned back, teetered on her shoulders. She watched the smile stretch across her face, her eyes close, and her lips part. And she wondered if something had happened in the meeting that maybe she shouldn't have missed. Or was Beatrice Newgarden having some sort of ailment that might need a doctor's attention?

She watched and waited. She had never imagined that this woman might have a mystical side to her. And it surprised her to think that someone had sat in silence in the basement of the church and felt the call of angels. Maybe the older woman was expecting her preacher to pray; she wondered what kind of prayer might be appropriate for the kitchen after a meal.

Beatrice snapped open her eyes like an exclamation point and nodded at the preacher. At the ceiling. At the angels. Charlotte couldn't be sure.

"Well, I guess that's all I need for this evening. I will see you on Sunday. Are you okay here locking up by yourself, or should I wait with you?"

"No," Charlotte assured her, "I'm used to being here alone. I need to go in my office for a few minutes anyway. You go ahead. I'll see you soon."

Beatrice filled her arms with her books and papers, the corner of her elbow weighted down by her purse. She turned as she walked out the back door. "Good night, dear."

"Good night, Mrs. Newgarden."

"It's Beatrice, dear, or Bea. You're my pastor, I think that allows you to be on a first-name basis, don't you?" She smiled and waved with two fingers on her left hand.

Charlotte laughed at the thought of this woman. Her crazy ideas, her need to keep things alive. Louise Fisher was right, she was a worrisome creature. But she had honorable intentions, and her heart was open, and sometimes that meant a lot more than good sense or a clear mind. She was harmless, even better, she was deliberate with her sweetness. Even when she baked her meddlesome prune cakes, she did it without a string attached. This, Charlotte understood, was plenty to be appreciated.

In the silence of the evening's close, the young pastor sat down and listened hard for what it was that Beatrice Newgarden had heard. She almost desired to hear something different. But there were only the things she knew and the tight edge of sadness that wrapped fiercely around her heart. This, of course, could not be lightened or loosed, not even for the song of an angel.

Earnestine's Corn Relish

1½ cups sugar
½ tablespoon salt
½ tablespoon celery seed
1 teaspoon dry mustard
1½ cups vinegar
1 teaspoon hot sauce
Two 15-ounce cans whole-kernel golden
    sweet corn
One 1½-ounce jar chopped pimiento
⅓ cup finely chopped onion
1 cup chopped green bell pepper

Heat sugar, salt, celery seed, mustard,
vinegar, and hot sauce. Bring the
ingredients to a boil and let boil for 2
minutes. Remove from heat, stir in corn,
pimiento, onion, and pepper. Cover and
cool. Place in refrigerator for several days to
allow relish to blend. Serves 8 to 10.

—EARNESTINE WILLIAMS

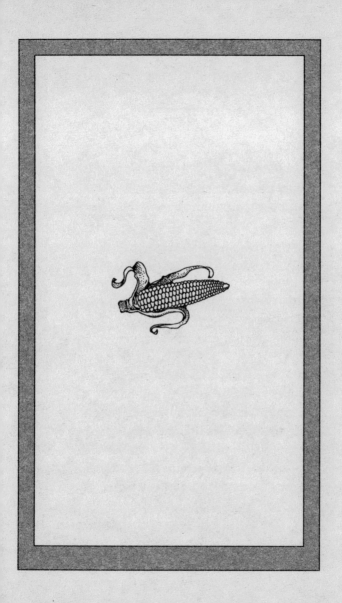

*I*t was Earnestine Williams who saw the cars hurry in and out of Louise's driveway. There were at least three cars with license plates from Maryland and one from Georgia or Florida. Earnestine had just happened by when she saw all the commotion. She had her son pull off the road onto Louise's yard just to make sure somebody wasn't stealing everything in her house. When she saw Louise come to the front door and wave her away, a signal that everything was okay, Earnestine became very curious and decided to call some of the other women to find out what they knew.

Once she got home and had a perfect view from her kitchen window, she saw five matching suitcases being taken in, a couple of boxes, and one apparently disoriented woman being supported on both sides by two large, strapping boys, followed by a couple of young women and one older man. Earnestine couldn't be sure if this woman was just old or sick or sick and old. But she watched as Louise stood holding open the door, her face twisted in a knot. Earnestine didn't think her neighbor had any elderly family left, certainly not any relatives in Maryland, and with an appropriate show of concern and worry, she called Margaret to see if she knew what was happening across the street.

Margaret was as cryptic as ever. Before Earnestine knew what had happened, Margaret had changed the subject, taking her mind off the important issue at hand. And not only was she waved away from the talk she desired but Earnestine was conned into taking nursery duty for two more Sundays, all because Margaret wouldn't answer any of her questions about Louise's affairs. In not so many words, Earnestine was told to mind her own business. And she vowed to herself for the hundredth time that she wouldn't call Margaret again.

Everybody knew that you shouldn't call Margaret for gossip. She just didn't have it in her to comment on the affairs of others. It was, for her, a task for someone else's mind. She simply was not going to participate. However, unlike her attitude toward the regular gossipy phone calls, Margaret became concerned after this one from Earnestine. She knew that it was Roxie who was staying with Louise, and, despite her typical uncanny ability to stay detached from the problems and issues of others, she wondered whether or not Louise was doing the right thing taking an Alzheimer's patient into her home. She decided not to give in to these unfamiliar leanings, wait a couple of days, and then she would, as she was prone to do, stop by and check on her friend.

It was thus, early in the dance of autumn, when the leaves just began to open themselves wide to the colors of nature and the sun edged farther away from the tilting earth, that Roxie Ann Barnette Cannon moved in with her best friend, Louise. It had been suggested and requested by first one and then another member of the family, until they finally all agreed that this arrangement might be best.

Louise had begged Roxie to come back to North Carolina. But Roxie, in her occasional moments of clarity, wished for things to be the same, and that meant living at home with her husband and their carefully planned out lives. When she wasn't clear, which was now most of the time, she showed no connection to any place or person or sentimentality.

George had neither the initiative nor the aptitude to care for his wife. And the children, busy in their own lives, wanted to take her but knew it simply could never work for one reason or another. Louise was the only one who sincerely wanted and knew how to care for their wife and mother. So they decided and agreed to let this happen.

After two days and all the family members having gone back to the lives they had put on hold to make this living change, Louise sat in the rocking chair pushed up against the window, watching Roxie sleep behind the bars of the hospital bed they had rented. The sleeping woman's mouth curled and twisted, her eyebrows knitted and released as if she were in the process of making a very important decision. Her facial muscles jerked, showing a struggle, and Louise felt a tear spill from her eye. She did not know how long she had been sitting there, but she was somewhat relieved when the doorbell rang and she saw Margaret standing on her front porch.

"Brought you some late corn, Lou. I hope you aren't tired of the summer vegetables yet." Margaret waited without coming in. She was not the pushy type.

Opening wide the door, Louise softened at her neighbor's presence. "Come in," she said.

Almost too inviting, thought Margaret.

"No, I quit getting corn weeks ago, and I'm not going to pay those supermarket prices for puny vegetables brought up here from Florida." Louise took the bag. "Come on in, I have some tea fixed. Care for a glass?"

"Thank you, I believe that would be just right." Margaret moved into the den with a bit of awkwardness. Even pushed against the far wall, the hospital bed and Roxie could not be ignored.

"I can't remember, do you take lemon?" Louise was in the kitchen.

"It doesn't matter. Whatever's easy." Margaret walked over to the bed and peered in at the woman she knew was Louise's greatest secret. Roxie now seemed to be sleeping like a child, all rolled up and comforted.

"She takes a nap every afternoon, before supper." Louise peeked around the corner as she got ice from the freezer. "I have pages and pages of her daily routine. I'm not sure I'll ever learn it all or get it all right. But so far everything's been fine. I just haven't slept in a few nights is all. I can't seem to leave the room yet for any length of time." She brought Margaret her tea and sat back down in the rocking chair.

Margaret sat on the sofa across the room. There was a long pause before she asked the question: "What are you doing, Lou?"

Louise bristled at first, ready to pounce in her own defense, but then she realized it wasn't Twila or Earnestine or any other nosy neighbor looking for a story. It was Margaret. It was her friend, and she put down her glass and walked over to the bed.

"She sleeps so peacefully in the afternoon, better than at night. There's something about the light, I guess, that eases her." She pulled the blanket around the sleeping woman's shoulders and continued to talk without looking at her neighbor.

"I met Roxie when we were both young and innocent." She stopped and turned to Margaret. "If you can believe there was such a day for me." She laughed and turned back to Roxie.

"And on the third day that we came home from the mill together and sat on the front porch of Mrs. Bonner's boardinghouse, drinking colas and laughing at the boss, I gave her my heart. I never said a word, of course." Louise unlatched the side rail of the bed and gently slid it down.

"I never asked a thing from her, but I was lost in her just the same, and I never found my way back to who I was before the day I promised myself to her." Louise pulled the covers over Roxie's shoulders.

"I suspect she knew I wasn't a 'safe' friend to be around. But it never seemed to matter. She loved me pure and hard in all the ways that she knew how. And I owe her everything of the goodness I have. She is the best part of me. She is that tiny place that hasn't closed in my heart. The only place inside me that isn't callous. So I know that I have waited my entire life to be able to give something back to her." She touched Roxie's cheek.

"And for the first time, the very first time in my life, I feel like I am exactly where I am supposed to be, exactly with the person I most want to be with, and doing the thing that is the most natural thing I could ever desire to do.

"I love her, Margaret." She turned around to face her friend. "Like you loved Luther and your father. Like Beatrice loves her causes. Like a mother loves her child. And I don't care that she doesn't know who I am or how much I love her. I know, and there is nothing, nothing else in this world that I want more to do than sit here by her side and care for her, feed her, sing to her, brush her hair, wipe her tears, clean her face, and read her stories."

Louise quit to catch her breath.

"Do you know, she can still talk about the mill and the boss and the boardinghouse like we were still there, in the beginning?"

Margaret had never seen Louise so un-guarded. She was a different woman altogether.

"I am so grateful that I get this chance finally to love her that I will cherish every single moment we have, like it was the very first moment I knew that I was alive." She stopped.

"Because that's what love is. That's what love does." Water stood in her eyes.

"That's what I'm doing, Margaret. I'm doing what love does." She turned back around and folded the sheet under Roxie's chin.

Margaret put down her head, embarrassed at

what had been said, embarrassed that she had asked, embarrassed that friendship wasn't always enough.

She waited, and then she stood up and walked next to Louise and put her arm around her shoulders, both of them looking into Roxie's face. "Then I will help you, Lou. I will love her too."

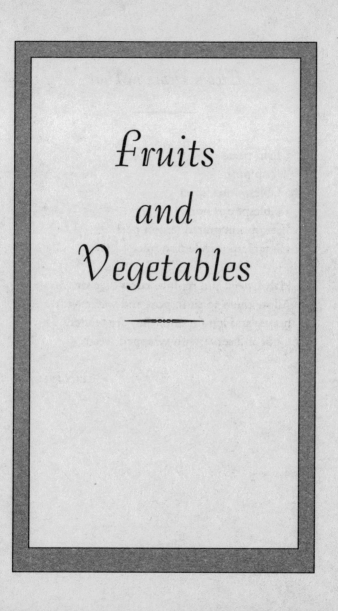

Fruits
and
Vegetables

Lucy's Pears in Port

3 firm pears
½ cup port
2 tablespoons water
3 tablespoons honey
½ teaspoon grated lemon peel
1 ½ tablespoons lemon juice

Halve, peel, and remove cores of pears.
Allow them to sit in port and water with
honey and lemon until they are tender.
Chill and serve with whipped cream.

—LUCY SEAL

"As the president of the Women's Guild, I would like to call this special meeting of the Cookbook Committee to order." Beatrice was rambling through her notes.

"Bea, it's just the five of us; I don't think Robert's Rules of Order are necessary. Jessie, do you want cream with your coffee?" Louise was hosting the meeting because it was easier to have folks come over to her house than to leave Roxie for any length of time. There were only a few people she trusted when she had to run errands, and after two months Roxie's condition had declined quite a bit. "Margaret, can you get some more napkins; they're in there next to the medicine bowl on the cabinet." She pointed to the kitchen with her chin.

Margaret got up from her seat and walked

into the kitchen. She was one of the few that Louise let stay with Roxie, and she could tell the situation had worsened. She also knew that Louise wasn't acknowledging the seriousness of things, but there didn't seem to be any way to approach it with her. She looked for the napkins, and there, sitting on the countertop, was a bowl filled with medicine bottles along with a schedule of what pill got taken at what time and a notebook filled with daily entries about Roxie. Margaret had only seen Louise make notes; she had never read what had been written, so she picked up the diary and began to flip through it.

Louise had notes about each meal, every bowel movement, Roxie's vitals, what she said, her facial expressions, what made her laugh, and what she remembered. There were copious explanations about every tick and blink Roxie made, and the sight of such obsessiveness concerned Margaret.

She had noticed a ferociousness in how Louise spoke about Roxie and the possibilities for curing Alzheimer's. She knew that Louise was determined to give Roxie a carefully planned diet that was filled with "brain food," like fish and garlic. She bought groceries like each meal was a sacred opportunity for healing, and she measured ingredients for Roxie's afternoon snacks like she was conducting a medical experiment. Margaret didn't realize until now how absorbed Louise was in making Roxie recover. She put down the book, found the napkins, and walked back into the den, where the committee was meeting.

"I still think if Lucy submitted a recipe for pears floating in wine, that's her business, and we don't have any right to censor it." Jessie had not seen the recipe, but everybody in church knew that Lucy Seal cooked with wine, usually a lot of wine.

Beatrice had opened the discussion of whether or not to ask Lucy to submit something other than her pears in port. "Well, I don't have a problem with an alcoholic beverage being mentioned in the cookbook, but I don't want the church to get a name for this."

"What name do you think we'd get, Bea?" Margaret was handing out the napkins.

"A church with no morals, a place that teaches their children that drinking is okay, a women's group that serves spiked punch at their meetings. I think there are all sorts of possibilities here, and why not just err on the side of caution and ask Lucy to give us another recipe?" Beatrice looked over at the preacher to see if she had any input, any suggestions, and secretly hoping that she would offer to deal with Lucy and this situation for the committee.

Charlotte suddenly felt Beatrice's eyes on her. She hadn't really been paying attention to what was being discussed, since she was observing Louise sitting beside Roxie on the bed. She watched as Louise took her pulse, wrote a note on a scrap of paper, and then brushed Roxie's hair back into a ponytail. She was whispering something into Roxie's ear, and it almost looked as if Roxie smiled. Louise made another note and helped Roxie up from the bed to walk back into the bathroom.

"Um, what's the recipe you're talking about?" Charlotte put down her coffee cup and smoothed her dress, trying to look interested.

"Lucy Seal gave us a recipe card for soaking pears in wine." Bea handed the preacher the copy of the recipe. "Do you think we should ask her to submit something different?" she asked, but the others looked for the preacher's answer as well.

"Did somebody else submit the same idea?" Charlotte took the paper, but she seemed confused.

Margaret smiled. "Bea's concerned about having alcohol mentioned in the church cookbook. Are you uncomfortable with that as the minister?"

Charlotte thought for a minute. She never drank. Once in college at a fraternity party, she had mistakenly picked up somebody else's glass loaded with vodka; she drank it before she knew what she had done. She didn't get drunk, but it had made her a little too uninhibited and she didn't like the way it left her feeling, loose and unprotected.

She was scared that her mother's genes had predisposed her to become an alcoholic. And since Serena had died from a drug overdose, it just seemed too likely that she would have the same disposition towards overindulgence. And yet, despite the problems with her mother, she never had a moral issue with drinking. After all, she had accepted the literal interpretation about

Jesus' lifestyle, which apparently had included the drinking of wine.

"Does the church have a written statement about alcohol use by its members?" she asked.

"No," Jessie said, crossing her arms over her chest. "We've never made a written statement about anything, but I'd have to guess that more than half the congregation would say that drinking is wrong."

"You think? Really, Jessie." Margaret looked surprised. "I guess I'm naive about some things. I would figure most of the folks have a bottle of wine sitting around the house and that nobody would really have a problem with fruit marinated in hooch."

Louise was coming up the hall with Roxie, who overheard the last bit of the conversation and began to yell, "Hooch, hooch, who's got the hooch?"

Everybody laughed.

"Not this bunch, Rox. This ain't the hooch type, if you know what I mean." Louise sat her on the bed and starting taking off her shoes.

"You drink hooch, Louie?" Roxie seemed clear.

Louise stopped and looked her in the face and

smiled. Roxie hadn't called her Louie since she had been in her house. "Oh yeah, I'm the queen of hooch."

Roxie tipped back her head and squealed. "You are the queen of hooch, Louie. Louie's the queen of hooch!" And she clapped her hands together while the women laughed with her.

"Louie, queen of hooch, huh? So that stuff we hear about Mrs. Bonner's boardinghouse in town is all true then?" Jessie was intrigued.

Roxie began to talk. "Oh, Louie could drink a fish out of its bowl. You remember the night we drove down to Fayetteville, Louie? You remember that drinking game you played with the soldiers?"

She looked away from Louise and at the other women. "Louie drank every parachute jumper under the table. She was the last one to vomit. Way to go, Louie!" Roxie stood up and pretended to give a toast.

"You must be so proud, Louise." Beatrice was enjoying the story and nodded back at Roxie with her coffee cup balanced on her palm.

"That was the night George gave me the ring, wasn't it, Louie? We had a fight, and then he showed up at the bar and gave me a diamond. So while I was getting hooked up you were getting hooched up."

All the women laughed.

"Good ole Louie, queen of the hooch." Roxie sat back on the bed, winded from the excitement.

"Yep, that's me! Good ole Louie."

Roxie reached over and gave Louise a hug. "Good ole Louie."

Louise took a tissue and wiped Roxie's nose. It was a bittersweet story that they were remembering.

Beatrice cleared her throat. Somebody had to break the spell. "Well, Louie," she said with a disapproving voice, "we still haven't made a decision about Lucy's recipe. I think Rev. Stewart should have the final word."

Charlotte pushed back a hair that had fallen into her face. "Then I say, keep it in. It's not worth hurting Mrs. Seal's feelings over it. If somebody gets upset about a fruit recipe, then we'll deal with it when it happens. But, really, I can't see much controversy about a cookbook." She picked up her cup and took a drink of coffee.

"Well, you should know by now that churches can have a controversy about anything. That Baptist church on King Road split over the picture behind the baptismal pool. Some thought Jesus should be coming out of the water, and some thought he should be going in. They had to go to court because the family paying for the painting got a lawyer. Split them right in two, and the lawyer is now the proprietor of the church."

Bea interrupted. "Well, I heard the preacher stirred everybody up by changing Sunday School from nine forty-five A.M. until after preaching. They say it was after that change that the whole baptismal pool incidence occurred." Bea raised her eyebrows and nodded at Jessie.

"So what are you saying, Bea, that altering the time of Sunday School made everybody stupid? This is the preacher's fault?" Margaret always cut to the chase.

Charlotte cut her eyes to Beatrice and listened closely.

"No, well, no, I'm just telling the whole situation of what happened, or at least the way I heard it." Bea was defensive but not rattled.

"That's the problem, Bea. The way you hear things is sometimes distorted." Margaret seemed to take this issue personally.

"Well, I've led us off on a tangent. Back to Lucy's recipe, I agree with you, Reverend. Besides, we aren't always intended to anticipate and prevent every conflict. Sometimes a good fight shakes a place up and reminds folks what's really important." Jessie nodded at Charlotte.

"Or nobody learns a thing and the lawyer ends up with the building." Margaret looked over at Beatrice. "Now what else is there, Bea?"

Bea looked down at her notes. "Well, somebody needs to decide about headings. Do we put the fruits with the vegetables or with the salads?"

"Vegetables." Roxie and Louise said it together. Louise looked at Roxie, unsure of how it could be that she was so clear. "Why vegetables, Rox?"

"Because it just sounds nicer. Now, I think I would like to give Ruby a call. Could you bring me the phone, dear?" Surprised at this sudden burst of clarity, Louise hurried out of the room and brought the cordless phone to Roxie. She dialed the number of Roxie's daughter and put the phone next to her ear, but Roxie had already fallen asleep. She pulled the phone away, listened for a minute as Ruby's machine picked up, then turned off the phone.

Louise stood up and spoke quietly but with excitement to the group. "Maybe the social activity of this committee helped her. Do you think that could be it? Do you think us being together and discussing instead of just me speaking to her helped her remember better?" She was talking very fast while she ran into the kitchen to get her notebook.

There was a pause. Margaret walked over to Roxie's bed while Louise came back into the room. "Louise, I really don't think there's any pattern to this. With Daddy, some days he just knew and some days he didn't. I don't think you can write down notes and figure this out." Margaret was taking off Roxie's glasses and putting her feet under the covers.

"Yeah, but did you hear her? She hasn't been this clear, well, not since she's come to stay with me. Maybe it was the talk about food. She loved to cook. She had tons of cookbooks. Maybe this conversation just brought her back to me."

Jessie began to clean up around where she was

sitting. "I once had an aunt who in her later years couldn't even tell you her name, but ask her a question about how to plant beans or when was the best time to harvest melons and she could be just as clear as a bell. She would know when the moon would be full and whether or not the tomatoes had enough lime in the soil." She shook her head. "It was that way right until she passed." Then she looked over at Louise as if she shouldn't have mentioned death, but Louise hadn't seemed to notice.

"Okay, well, it's getting late." Beatrice seemed uncomfortable. "I just have one more question." She was writing something down. "Is grits a vegetable or an old favorite?"

"Somebody gave a recipe for grits?" Margaret shook her head and looked over at the preacher, who shrugged her shoulders.

"Dorothy West said that her sister had a recipe for fried grits that would make your mouth water." Beatrice took her last sip of coffee.

"Who needs a recipe for fried grits?" Jessie asked. "You just take the leftover grits, put them in a loaf pan, and then put it in the icebox. When you take it out, you cut it into slices and dip them in flour and eggs, then you just stick them in the frying pan until they're done. Don't you do that with your leftover grits?"

The women looked at each other stunned. "No, I stick mine in the microwave with a little water," Margaret said.

"I don't eat grits," replied Louise.

"Well, don't look at me," Charlotte said. "I haven't ever cooked grits in my life."

The women smiled.

"We've been doing that with grits for as long as I can remember. I thought everybody around here knew about fried grits. I guess I was wrong. This cookbook is going to be a community culture lesson for us all."

"Jessie, speaking of Dorothy West, is Wallace doing some work over there?" Beatrice had sat back down with her books by her side. She had heard something. Everybody could tell. Margaret rolled her eyes.

"No," Jessie said with a knowingness of Beatrice's ways. "I think he's become friends with her granddaughter, Lana. They're in the same classes at school. He says she's better in science and he's better in English, so they help each other out. He's third in his senior class at the high school, you know. Janice is real proud of that boy, and so am I. He's gotten invitations to several of the colleges to come and visit, but I don't think he's made up his mind about what he wants to do or where he wants to go yet. Beatrice, since you've asked, do you have some concern about my grandson and who he spends time with?"

Beatrice fidgeted in her seat, pulled at her chin, and picked up her papers. "No, Jessie, I just wondered is all."

"Your wondering, Bea, is sure an awful lot like nosiness to me." Margaret was tired of the nonsense.

Beatrice rolled her eyes. "Well, you've got to know that people will talk."

"What will people talk about, Mrs. Newgarden, I mean, Beatrice?" Charlotte was curious to hear an explanation.

Beatrice looked around for someone else to answer, but Louise was busy filling in the pages of her notebook about Roxie, and Margaret and Jessie were staring at Beatrice, looking for an answer to the question.

"Oh, come on, there's no need to act naive, any of you. You all know what I'm talking about. Lana's white and Wallace is, well, Wallace is . . . ," she stammered.

"An A student," Margaret answered. "And a fine young man and Jessie's grandson. So I suggest that you tell any of your gossiping friends who feel the need to 'talk,' that two young people have the right to be friends and it's none of their concern to comment or even notice. And, furthermore, a young black man can be at a white person's house without doing manual labor in the backyard."

Jessie smiled and looked over at Beatrice, who was so stunned at Margaret's challenge that she kicked over her coffee cup. Charlotte stood to help her clean up her mess, and even Louise stopped writing to see what would happen next.

Roxie rolled over and began to talk. "No black people are allowed in the boardinghouse. It's Mrs. Bonner's only rule, but we can sneak her in the back when the old lady's gone to sleep." She yawned.

"Yeah, Rox, we can do that." Louise was at her side.

"We can do that," Roxie repeated.

"I'm sorry, Jessie. I had no right." Beatrice was flushed.

"It's okay, Bea. I knew the stuff that was being said. Years may roll by, but some things just never change." Jessie glanced towards the window.

There was an awkward pause.

Margaret walked over to Louise. "Lou, I need to talk to you about staying with Roxie tomorrow morning. Cleo's coming over to the house to check the chimney for bats. It's the only time he could come this week, and I have to be there to let him in. What time is your doctor's appointment?"

Louise closed her notebook. "It's at ten. But it's no big deal; I can reschedule."

"No, don't do that, Louise. Let me stay." It was Beatrice, and the offer surprised everyone.

Margaret and Louise looked at her, then at each other.

"You never let me stay. I can take care of Roxie for a couple of hours. What time do you need me?"

Louise stammered, trying to find the words to answer Beatrice. "Um, nine. I really don't have to go, though. I can get another time. It's just for my physical; I had scheduled it a long time ago, before, um, before Roxie came."

"Then you should keep it. It took me four months to get in to see Dr. Johnson. I waited for an hour, spent ten minutes with him, and paid a hundred and fifty dollars. Something's dreadfully wrong with our medical system. But, anyway, you need to keep that appointment, and I'll be back in the morning at eight thirty so you can go over any instructions. It will be fine."

Louise tried to respond, but before she could think of anything to say, Beatrice had put her cup on the table, cleaned up around her seat, picked her belongings, said good-bye to everyone, and headed out the door.

"What just happened?" Louise asked.

"Beatrice is paying for her sins," Jessie replied as she gathered her things. "She's actually trying to be your friend. It will be good for both of you to let her stay. Don't you think, Margaret?"

Margaret raised her eyebrows and nodded.

"Well, I better go. Thank you for the goodies, Lou." Jessie walked into the kitchen and back into the den.

"Margaret, Reverend, have a good evening. We'll see you Sunday." She went over and spoke a few words to Roxie, then left.

"Well, Cookbook Committee meetings certainly aren't boring," Charlotte said. "Ms. Fisher—"

Louise interrupted her. "It's Louise, dear."

"Louise, you're doing a great job caring for your friend. If you need anything from the church, just let me know. Good night, you two."

"Here, I'll walk out with you." Margaret kissed Louise on the cheek. "I'll talk to you tomorrow."

Louise shut and locked the door behind them, picked up the other cups and plates, and placed them in the sink. She turned out the kitchen light and hurried back into the den. She opened up the diary and began to write: "The Cookbook Committee met tonight. Roxie knew who I was, talked about the night in Fayetteville, remembered her daughter. I think there may be some improvement in her condition." She dated the entry, changed into her pajamas, and came back to sit next to Roxie as she slept.

Louise rocked in the chair next to the bed

with a blanket pulled up around her shoulders, fighting sleep. Despite her attempts to convince herself that she was staying for Roxie's sake, she was really hoping for just one more word.

Dorothy's Fried Grits

You must do some of this recipe ahead of time.
1 cup grits
4 cups water
Flour
2 eggs, beaten in a bowl

Cook grits in water. Pour them into a loaf pan and place in the refrigerator. After a couple of hours, cut the grits into slices. Dip them in flour, then eggs, then back into flour again. Fry in grease until brown.

—DOROTHY WEST

Margaret was surprised when she got home and found Lana Sawyer, Dorothy West's granddaughter, on the porch, sitting on the steps. She parked the car in the garage and walked around front.

"It's getting late, Lana. Don't you have school tomorrow?"

"Yes, ma'am, but I can go later because my first class is study hour. I need to talk to someone. I need to talk to you."

"Does your mom know where you are? Do you need to call home?" Margaret was unlocking the front door.

"No. I don't have to be home until eleven. They're used to me being out late." Lana walked in the house.

Margaret closed the door and led the girl into

the kitchen. "Want a soda or something? I have juice and cola and cocoa, if you'd like something hot."

"Yeah, cocoa sounds good." She sat down at the table. She was holding her stomach.

Margaret noticed and knew. Lana had to be more than four or five months along. How could no one have noticed? she wondered to herself. She heated up the milk while they talked about school and the teachers. Then Margaret mixed the cocoa with sugar and put it in two mugs.

"I'm pregnant." Lana said this as she stirred her hot drink.

"Yes." This was Margaret's only reply. She pulled out a chair and sat down next to the young girl.

"It's Wallace Jenkins's. We've been seeing each other for almost a year." She took a deep breath, blew across the hot chocolate, and put the mug to her lips.

"Who knows?" Margaret took a sip herself.

"Wallace, of course. He's trying to figure out what to do. My best friend, Tina, and I'm pretty sure her mom knows. And I told the guidance counselor, Ms. Oakley. I haven't had the nerve to tell my family yet. My mom and grandmother are going to have a cardiac."

"How far along are you? Have you been to the clinic?" Margaret knew that a lot of girls went across town when this sort of thing happened.

"No. I guess I didn't really believe it for a while. But I haven't had a period in almost four months. I've been real sick too. Mama just thinks it's a virus."

"Yep, it's a virus all right." Margaret smiled.

"What do you think, Mrs. Peele? What should I do?"

Margaret didn't say anything for a few minutes. She was studying the girl. It seemed that already the pregnancy had aged her, not just physically but emotionally, maybe even spiritually. Lana was changed from the young girl she had been in Margaret's Bible classes. Already the weight of motherhood was filling up her heart, changing her vision of the world.

Margaret could see it. Lana had been empty in one moment and filled up in the next. She faced a future unlike one she had ever anticipated, and Margaret was sizing her up to see if she had what it took.

Lana caught Margaret's eye. "What you looking for, Ms. Peele?"

"Courage, I guess." She peered more deeply.

"And? Do you see any?" Lana seemed nervous about the answer.

Without a pause Margaret replied loud and strong, as if the very response made a difference. "Oh yes, child, I see lots of courage." She reached up and brushed her hand across Lana's cheek. "Your being here, that took courage. Your letting Wallace be a part, that's brave too." She cupped her hands around Lana's. "You're going to be a great mother; I can tell these things, you know."

Lana's eyes filled with tears, and for a brief moment she was a child again. Margaret leaned over and held her.

"Now, the first thing we need to do is get you to a doctor. Do you want me to take you, or do you want me to go with you to tell your mother tonight?"

Lana wiped her face on the napkin under her mug. "I think I need to tell her before I go to the doctor, but I want Wallace with me." She stopped and smiled. "He loves me, you know.

But his mother"—she blew a puff of air—"and his grandmother, God, they have such plans for him. They're always talking about him being the first Jenkins to go to an Ivy League school, the first Jenkins to be a doctor or lawyer. Believe me, father is not the role they had planned for him." She teared up and looked away.

"Young Wallace can still be anything he wants to be, as can you, my dear. And Janice and Jessie, they're good women. They'll come around." She patted Lana on the hand. "What are your feelings for Wallace? Do you love him, Lana?"

Lana turned back to look at Margaret. "I think so. I mean, I haven't really dated a lot of guys." She took a sip. The cocoa had cooled down. "I'm not sure. We've been friends for as long as I can remember. He knows everything about me. He's funny and smart, and he's the best person I've ever known. You know what I mean, he just always does the right thing. I love that about him."

She stopped and pulled the mug of cocoa closer to her.

"I think I love him, but Mama, she just can't accept that he's black. So I don't know. I feel like

I have to choose between my family and him. I've always felt like that, even when we were just friends."

Margaret nodded. "Well, that baby didn't get to choose, so we're just going to have to find a way that you don't either. And if your family forces you to make a decision like that, then you'll choose love, however that looks, whoever that's with. You'll choose love because that's more important than anything, especially for a baby."

Lana put down the mug and rubbed her stomach as if to make the words sink in. Her eyes were filled with tears.

"Now," Margaret said, looking at the wall clock. "We better go over and pick up Wallace and get to your mother's house before she goes to bed."

Lana wiped her eyes again, brushed back her hair, pulled her chair away from the table, and stood up. "I think I'll call Wallace first, you know, let him know I'm going to do this."

"Sounds like a good idea to me. The phone's by the fridge, there on the wall." Margaret got up from her chair and took the mugs to the sink.

She tried not to listen to the girl's conversation, but it was hard to avoid eavesdropping.

"I'm at Ms. Peele's. No"—she looked towards Margaret at the sink—"she's cool. We're going to tell Mom. I want you to go with me." There was a pause. "About fifteen minutes. Okay, we'll meet you there." She turned away from Margaret and faced the wall. "Me too." And she hung up the phone.

"He'll meet us at my house. I think he's going to tell his grandmother before he goes. I'm sure relieved that I don't have to be there for that one." Lana walked over to the sink and stuck her hands under the faucet. She dried them on the towel Margaret handed her. "I'm really glad you're going with me. My mom respects you. She won't lose it too bad if you're there."

"Yes, I guess she'll remember that I was her Sunday School teacher too. I have a few stories about your mother when she was your age." Margaret folded the towel and set it on the kitchen counter. "If things start to get a little out of hand, I'll pull one or two out of my memory bank and shake things up a little."

Lana nodded her head and smiled.

"So, you ready to go?" Margaret picked up her keys and opened the back door.

The young woman looked around the kitchen as if she would be different the next time she came into the room. Then she nodded. "Okay, here goes nothing!" She walked out the door as Margaret turned out the light and followed her.

The ride from Margaret's to Dorothy's daughter's house was quiet as the two women tried to put their thoughts into the words they were going to say. Margaret wondered about how it must sound to a mother that her little girl is pregnant, if such news can really break a heart. She thought about her place in this mess and why it was she had been given such an honorable role among the young people in the community. She thought about her own barrenness and what it meant to her not to have children.

She and Luther had had only one conversation about the fact that there were no children. And one question, with an answer of "I don't know" hardly qualifies for a conversation.

They had been married thirteen years when Margaret finally mustered the courage to ask. "Why do you think I haven't gotten pregnant?" Luther paused for a moment, then picked up the newspaper and sat down at the table. "I don't know" was all he said. And because she was busy enough with the farm and looking after her dad and because she wasn't even sure she really wanted her own children, she had not pursued it any further.

When Luther died and his sister, Carolyn, commented that it was a crying shame there were no children to share this tragedy, Margaret thought it odd that she did not even consider not having children as another reason to mourn. Perhaps because her mother died when she was such a young girl, Margaret had not ever had the space to entertain notions of what being a mother was like.

She was not regretful and had never grieved that she did not have children. And somehow she imagined that the girls came to her in their darkest moments of discontent because she would never automatically take their mothers' side or present the fear or protectiveness that a mother always harbors. She was a safe and reliable ally. She was a wise and trusted friend. And to Margaret this was better than being someone's mother.

When they pulled into the driveway, Wallace

was already there; he was sitting in his car. Margaret watched as the young man opened the door and stood as his grandmother got out from the passenger's side.

"Well, I guess this is it then. You ready?" Margaret turned and faced Lana.

"I'm a mother now. Courage will be the most important thing I can give my child." Lana gazed towards Wallace. "After love, of course." She faced Margaret, who replied, "Of course."

They got out of the car, and Lana walked over to Wallace. Immediately they embraced, spoke to each other privately, and walked to the front porch.

"Beats all, doesn't it?" Jessie shut the car door, watching the two young people as they walked past her. Lana looked her in the eye and then dropped her face.

"Are you very disappointed, Jessie?" Margaret put her hand on Jessie's arm.

"Oh, I guess a little. This isn't anything to throw a party about." She sighed deeply. "But I still believe in that boy. And he's handling this like a real man. I am proud of him for that. He intends to be a father to that child, even though he doesn't have a clue what that means."

Margaret nodded. "I know. I don't think anyone really realizes what all that encompasses, do
they? But, you know, these two kids have a lot
already on their side. They've got you. And
Lana's mom, she'll be upset at first, but she'll get
over the initial shock and be there for them. Janice will support the two of them. She's your
daughter, after all."

Jessie interrupted. "And they've got you. And
I know what I'm talking about now, you're the
best friend a young couple or even a grandmother can have. Yeah, we'll do okay," she said as
they joined Wallace and Lana at the door, "we'll
all do just fine."

She reached up and held Lana's chin in her
hand. "My grandson loves you, Lana Sawyer.
That counts for a whole lot in his grandmother's
record book. You're family now. The Jenkins and
Sawyer blood is mingled in that baby's heart. I'm
going to stand by you, you and your child. I will
never turn my back on family."

Lana threw her arms around Jessie, almost
knocking her off the porch. "Thank you, Mrs.
Jenkins. I was so afraid."

"Well, I reckon you still got one more bridge
to cross with your family. And since we're here,

and your grandmother's looking out the bedroom window, we better not stop." They all glanced towards the back bedroom, where the curtains quickly fell back together.

Lana and Wallace both took in deep breaths. Margaret rang the bell. The door opened, and they all walked in.

Peggy's Fried Okra

4 cups okra (cut crosswise)
Flour
4 slices fried bacon, coarsely chopped
Bacon drippings
2 cups peeled and chopped tomatoes
Salt and pepper

Cut okra crosswise and flour. Cook bacon.
Fry okra in bacon drippings until brown.
Add tomatoes to okra, stir in bacon. Season
to taste. Simmer until tomatoes are tender.
Stir often.

—PEGGY DUVAUGHN

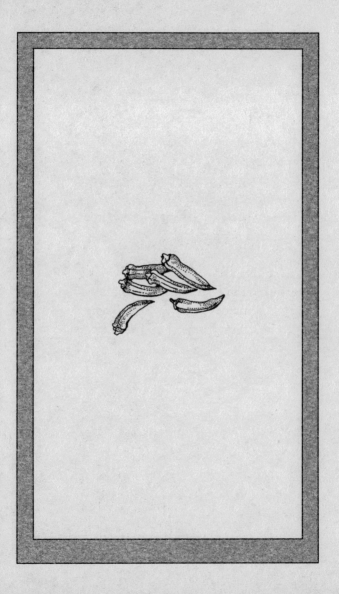

The doorbell was ringing and Louise was trying to get Roxie's clothes on her. Breakfast had been a catastrophe because Roxie kept saying that she was being poisoned and wouldn't eat anything put in front of her. Louise had tried oatmeal, eggs, even a cinnamon coffee cake. It was just going to be a bad day, and, as bad days went, nothing was going to change that. Louise left Roxie with her pants hanging around her knees and went to the door.

"Come in, Bea. We're having a difficult morning." Louise started walking back towards the hospital bed. "Roxie thinks the milk is rat bait and her blouse is a straitjacket. She's fighting against everything." She turned to Bea, who was following behind. "Maybe I should call and cancel the appointment. She can be a real handful when she's like this." Louise sat down in the chair next to the bed. Roxie was trying to take off her underwear.

"Nonsense. I mothered three children. I think I can handle things just fine." Bea walked in the room and put her things on the coffee table. She took a look around, at the room, at the window, at the hospital bed, and finally at Roxie. "Good morning, Roxie. I'm Beatrice. Are you having a bad morning with Louise?" Bea went and knelt down in front of Roxie.

"They're trying to kill me. Where's the supervisor? He won't put up with this nonsense." She stood up and almost knocked Beatrice down.

Beatrice thought for a moment. "Well, the supervisor sent me here to check on things. I'm sort of like the assistant to the supervisor. You can tell me all about the problems, but first I think you need to put your clothes on." Beatrice picked up the blouse and pants. Roxie folded her arms about her waist and showed a determination for staying naked. Beatrice waited a minute, still standing with Roxie's clothes in her arms, smiled at her, and then, much to Louise's surprise, Roxie let Beatrice put them on her. There was no struggle at all.

Finally Beatrice asked, "Now, why is someone trying to kill you? Do you know something you're not supposed to know?" she whispered. "Have you done something that's made them mad?"

Roxie looked serious. She was giving great thought to the questions. "I think it's about the red thread. I took some of the red thread." She spoke very softly. "I think they know."

Beatrice whispered in reply. "Then we'll put some red thread back so they won't miss it." She turned to Louise. "Do you have any red thread?"

Louise was baffled by this entire exchange. She sat watching until Beatrice spoke her name; then she jumped. "Um, yeah, sure." And she went into another room, brought back a spool of red thread, and handed it to Beatrice, who gave it to Roxie. Roxie started to cry.

Beatrice sat beside her on the bed and rocked her. "There, there, Roxie. See, we have plenty of red thread. It's okay. Nobody's ever going to try to hurt you again." Then she reached over for a tissue and gave it to Roxie, who wiped her own eyes and nose.

"Well, Louise, you better tell me if there are any particular instructions I need to know, and then you need to hurry and get dressed."

Louise looked down at her khaki pants bought from the men's department at Sears and the University of North Carolina sweatshirt. She thought she was dressed. "Actually, Bea, this is what I'm wearing to the doctor's, but, you're right, I do need to get going."

Louise began looking for her shoes. "She usually naps after breakfast and then has a snack around ten thirty. She takes the orange pill then. I don't put a diaper on her during the day because generally she can tell me when she needs to go. But it's always a gamble. Snack is a piece of fruit or peanut butter crackers." Louise walked into the kitchen with Beatrice close behind her.

"Here's the ten-thirty pill. It's a vitamin really. But I think they help her memory a little. There's juice in the fridge. The fruit is in the small Tupperware dishes, and the crackers are there on the counter. She didn't eat breakfast, so she may want both this morning. She really doesn't eat much, though." Louise was trying to remember everything important.

"Here's the doctor's number." She wrote the number on a pad of paper.

"I may stop by the bank on my way home. But don't worry about lunch. I'll be home by

twelve thirty at the latest." She tore off the paper
and put down the pad near Beatrice's arm. "And
if you don't mind, just jot down her intake and
the things that she says. I like to keep a record."

"Well, it all seems easy enough. Now you run
along, and we'll be fine." Beatrice opened the
door for Louise, who stood as if she was waiting
for something.

"Are you sure you're going to be okay?"

Beatrice rolled her eyes and said in a motherly
tone, "We'll be fine."

"Let me just go and say good-bye." Louise
went back into the den.

Beatrice stayed by the door while Louise ex-
plained to Roxie that she was only going to the
doctor's and would be right back. Roxie seemed
uninterested in Louise's plans and began counting the birds in the backyard. Louise came back
into the kitchen, grabbed her wallet. "Thank
you, Bea. I'll be back as soon as I can."

"It's fine. Take your time. We'll be here all
day." Beatrice almost pushed Louise through the
screen door. "Bye, bye now!" She waved briefly,
then shut the door.

Louise stood on the porch, suddenly feeling
like a stranger. She considered not going to the

doctor's at all but going back inside and telling
Beatrice that her "services" were not needed.
But she knew that that was being silly, and that
she really needed a break from being in the
house with Roxie alone. Sometimes the con-
stant fighting made her weary. She walked to the
car, got in, and headed off to her appointment as
planned.

When she got to the office, she checked in
with the receptionist. Peggy DuVaughn was in
the waiting room, and when she saw Louise she
called her over to sit beside her.

"Are you okay, Louise?" Peggy was curious
but, for the most part, harmless.

"Oh sure. Just my annual physical. You?"

"I'm here with Vastine. I expect the fluid's
built up around his heart again. The doctor will
probably have to drain it. I hope they don't have
to put him in the hospital. It's so hard on him
when he goes." She looked down at her watch.
"Which doctor do you see?"

Louise found the conversation annoying and
considered the possibility that she should call
home and check on Beatrice and Roxie, even
though she had been gone only fifteen minutes.
"Um, Dr. Phillips. She's new, I guess."

"Yes, I believe she is. Do you like her?"

"She's fine. What time do you have, Peggy?" Louise was fidgety.

"Nine fifty. Is your appointment at ten?"

"Yeah. I hope they're on time." She picked up a magazine.

"Oh, I think so at this hour in the morning. It's those afternoon appointments that are so far behind. People calling in sick, you know, needing to come in today. Forget about the fact that others have been waiting for hours. And those regular visits that they thought would only take fifteen minutes suddenly taking an hour. And then there's the emergencies!" She paused. "Louise, are you sure you're okay? You look a little flushed."

Louise sighed. "I'm fine." She stopped, then continued. "It's just Beatrice is watching Roxie for me, and it's their first time alone together." She put down the magazine.

Peggy patted her on the arm. "Oh, they'll be fine. Beatrice is a good nurse. She stayed with Vastine once when I got the shingles and he was in the hospital. You don't need to worry; besides, she knows where you are, right? If something goes wrong, she'll call."

Louise began to think about what could go wrong. A fire or a break-in. There were possibilities she hadn't thought of.

"Oh look, there's Lilly Andrews." Peggy waved in the direction of a woman at the reception desk. "Hi, Lilly."

Peggy whispered, "She's got cancer, you know. It's so sad."

Louise looked at the woman, who was waving back to them. She had a pink-and-white turban on her head.

"By the way," Peggy said, "I have my cookbook recipe in my purse. I was planning to mail it to Margaret, but since you're here and on that committee, I'll just give it to you."

"Maybe you should just mail it to Margaret. I'm a little scattered and might misplace it." Louise could feel her blood pressure rising. How long can this doctor's appointment take? she wondered.

"Nonsense. Just stick it in your purse. Besides, it will save me a stamp." She pulled the envelope from her purse.

"Look, I'd rather give you money for the stamp than be responsible for keeping up with the thing. Send it to Margaret, please." Louise got up from her seat and went to ask the receptionist how long it would be before she saw the doctor. She brushed past the woman with cancer. When she got back, Peggy looked upset and didn't speak. Louise knew she had hurt her feelings.

"Peggy, I'm sorry. Give me the recipe; I'll give it to Margaret." Louise stuck her hand out.

"No, it's obviously an inconvenience for you, so I'll mail it this afternoon like I planned." She pushed Louise's hand away. "Besides, there's Vastine, so I'll be going now." She got up and walked towards the desk to check out. "Vastine," she called out. "I'm over here." Her husband looked over towards her voice.

"Peggy, wait. Look, I'm sorry." Louise followed her, trying to make amends. "Is it for your fried okra? I love that. With the tomatoes and the bacon drippings? I'd like my own copy of that recipe." Louise tried but failed to regain Peggy's attention. She had gone over to Lilly and was speaking to her.

Great, Louise thought, now I've pissed her off. But before she could get to her or decide what to do, the nurse came out and called Louise's name.

After an X ray and blood test, Dr. Phillips came in the examining room where Louise was waiting and looked over her file. She poked and prodded a few body parts, then sat down on the stool in front of the examining table. The doctor, who had taken Roxie as a patient, knew about Louise's living situation. She asked how they were both doing together. Having noticed Louise's high blood pressure and her agitated state, she began to try to tell Louise that she would have to get some help. She waited a minute, then suggested a home health nurse. Louise made no response.

Dr. Phillips then brought up the possibility of nursing home placement, which sent Louise into a rage, so she backed away from that idea but still encouraged her to look into home health agencies, and Louise finally agreed.

"You do understand, don't you, Ms. Fisher, that things are only going to get worse? Roxie's condition will decline, and I don't believe that you are going to be able to care for her on your own."

Louise waved aside the advice and asked if they were finished. The doctor shook her head in frustration, wrote a prescription for blood pressure pills, told Louise to have her pressure checked regularly, and to come back in one month. She also wrote an order for a home health nursing assessment and handed the papers to Louise. As she was going out the door, Louise stopped her. "How long does she have, Doctor?"

Dr. Phillips turned around. She went back to the stool and sat down. She studied Louise, then she began. "Alzheimer's doesn't allow for a complete prognosis. All we know is the condition of the patient continues to worsen. Bodily functions just break down. There's no way of knowing how long somebody can live with the disease." She paused for a moment. "But I do know that in the end stages one person can't do all of the caregiving. You'll have to have some help." She looked at Louise. "Do you understand, Ms. Fisher? You can't care for Roxie by yourself."

Louise dropped her head. She wiped her eyes, took a deep breath. "Thank you." And with that the doctor nodded and left the room.

It was the news that Louise held somewhere inside her. The familiar ring from what Roxie's family had told her months ago. She knew it, tried to keep it in the front of her mind as she was carrying out the day-to-day tasks, but taking it deep inside, digesting it, letting it be a part of her soul, was something she couldn't do. It seemed to her that it was like a foreign body, this bad news, and that her system was doing what it was made to do, fight it, hold it back, keep it from coming in, infecting everything, and taking over. It felt more natural to struggle against it, ignore and deny it, than to deal with it.

Louise had never known such turmoil. With the others she knew who had gone through a time of dying, it had been different. It hurt, but it never split her heart. Not like this. This time it felt like a disease. Until now she didn't know emotional pain could alter the pressure of the circulation of her blood, change the number of times her heart beat in a minute, cause her shoulders to feel tied together and the back of her head to burn. She thought she had known suffering before, but nothing, nothing had ever been like this.

Louise got dressed, paid her bill, and left the doctor's office. Before going by the bank, she went to the pharmacy and was back home at just a little after twelve. It seemed unusually quiet as she opened the door and went inside. She thought that Roxie's nap had gone a little late. She put her things on the counter, called out for Beatrice, and walked into the den. In only a matter of minutes, the room had become a war zone.

In the lull of the late morning, Beatrice had fixed Roxie's hair and put makeup on her so that, while sleeping, she looked like a made-up corpse lying in a casket. She lay there with her hands folded across her chest and the sheet pulled just under her chin. Louise went into a fit.

"Oh, dear God! Rox, Roxie, wake up! Jesus! I was only gone a couple of hours! How did this happen? Roxie, Rox!" She knocked everything off the coffee table jumping on the bed. "You can't be dead! Oh, God, please don't let it be so!" Louise was straddled over Roxie, shaking her by the shoulders, hugging her, crying and yelling.

Beatrice ran from the bathroom up the hall, her dress still hiked up from having been on the toilet. "My God, what's happened?" She was screaming as well.

"She's dead! Lord help me, Roxie's dead!"

It was flying elbows and knees. Heads and necks jerking. Bodies stretched into bodies.

Louise was pulling on Roxie while Beatrice was pulling on Louise.

"Lou, Louise." Beatrice was trying to gain control. She had Louise by the back of her sweatshirt, trying to get her off the bed, but Louise was stronger than Beatrice.

"She's dead. O Lord, my Roxie." And then the words melted into cries and sobs. Louise had Roxie's body up and in her arms so tightly that when Roxie finally was able to move it was only with her feet. She kicked as hard as she could, but all she did was force Beatrice off the bed and onto the floor, her dress now up around her waist.

Finally, Louise eased her grip on Roxie and was kicked out of the bed herself, falling squarely on top of Beatrice. Roxie began to yell, "You're killing me! She's killing me. I told you, Ms. Bea, they're trying to kill me." But when she looked down and saw Louise sprawled out on Beatrice, who was fighting with her dress and with Louise to get up, she began to laugh. She laughed so hard that she started to hiccup. And when Beatrice and Louise were finally able to grasp the situation, they began to laugh too.

It seemed like a long time before Louise was

able to pull herself off the floor, but when she did she bent down and gave Beatrice a hand.

"What the devil is wrong with you?" Beatrice was tugging at the hand and at her dress at the same time. "What on earth made you go all crazy all of a sudden?"

Louise began to straighten herself up a little while Roxie was still laughing. "Why did you put that mess on her face and fix her hair like that?"

Roxie answered, "We played beauty parlor, didn't we, Ms. Bea? She even did my toenails." And she pulled her feet from under the sheets and wiggled her toes.

"I just put a little makeup on her and did her hair up. She seemed to like it." Beatrice was still shaky from the whole experience. "I never thought, not for a moment, that you would think, well, that you could imagine . . ." She could not even finish her sentence.

"It was beauty parlor stuff, Louie. Ms. Bea just let me go to the beauty parlor. Don't you think I look nice?" She had reached over and put her arm around Louise, who was sitting beside her on the bed.

"You look great, Rox. Real pretty." Louise

moved a loose hair from Roxie's forehead back to where it had come from. She looked over at Beatrice. "I'm sorry," she said as sincerely as she could. "I overreacted. Way overreacted. I don't know, I just went a little crazy or something."

Beatrice touched up her own hair, tapped herself lightly on the neck. "It's okay. Everything's fine." She blew out a breath. "But really, Louise, what on earth were you thinking?"

"Yeah, no, I don't know. I'm sorry. Really, I'm sorry." She began to put things back on the coffee table.

Roxie continued to laugh at the situation as Louise tried to straighten things up.

"Bea, you'll stay for lunch, won't you? I'll fix us something." Louise was picking up papers and coasters.

"Ms. Bea stays for lunch. It would be a pleasure." Roxie smiled at Beatrice.

Beatrice waited for a minute while both Louise and Roxie stared at her. "Well, all right. But I can't think that I'll have much of an appetite after this ordeal." She fanned herself with a magazine that had been at her feet. "Do you need me to do anything?"

"No," said Louise. "I'll handle it. You two can

just stay in here." She went into the kitchen while Beatrice and Roxie began to play through the scene over and over. They were making fun of Louise screaming, "She's dead . . . Dear God, she's dead!"

Louise yelled from the kitchen, "Yeah, that's really funny, you two." And they laughed some more.

After lunch Roxie took a nap and Louise and Beatrice began to clean up the dishes. They were mostly quiet until Beatrice asked, "So, was everything all right at the doctor's?"

Louise washed and rinsed a dish and handed it to Beatrice. "She says I need to get some help with Roxie pretty soon."

There was an awkward pause. "I can't stand the thought of a stranger caring for her." She handed Beatrice a cup. "But I also know I can't keep doing this by myself."

Beatrice said nothing. There was only the sound of splashing water.

"What, Ms. I Can Fix Everything doesn't have an answer?" Louise looked over at Beatrice. It was really only a joke.

Beatrice waited. "No. I have no answer for this." She put down the towel. "But I do know that when you love someone, a part of loving them is sharing them."

It was a strange and awkward moment. Beatrice put her hands on Louise's shoulders, turning her so they could look eye to eye. "There are folks who want to help you, Lou. Let us. We really won't kill her." She dropped her hands and picked up the towel. She dried a dish and put it in the cabinet. "Even if it looks like it."

Beatrice elbowed Louise in the ribs.

"Yeah?" Louise looked at Beatrice like it was the first time she'd seen her.

"Yeah."

Meats

Twila's Chicken Pie

CRUST
½ cup water
½ pound pure lard
3 cups flour
½ teaspoon salt
½ teaspoon baking powder

FILLING
2½ pounds cooked chicken
3 cups chicken broth
1 stick margarine
1½ cups milk
5 tablespoons cornstarch

Boil water and add to lard until lard is melted. Add flour, salt, and baking powder, mixing well. Roll into a ball and chill before using.

Cook chicken in lightly salted water. When tender, remove chicken from bones and cut into small pieces. Strain chicken broth, and measure 3 cups in a 3-quart pot. Add margarine and milk, bringing to the boiling point. Dissolve cornstarch in a small amount of cold water and add to the broth mixture, stirring constantly until a gravy is obtained. Salt and pepper to taste. Pour the chicken mixture into a 9 x 13 x 2-inch pan. Roll out the chilled crust and top the chicken mixture. Bake in a hot oven (400°F to 425°F) until brown. Serves 8.

—TWILA MARKS

*T*wila Marks was the first one to come right out and ask Charlotte about the wedding. The preacher felt the sanctuary rock and steady after Sunday worship when it was announced. She knew everybody was whispering about it at their cars, but no one said anything to her until Twila.

She claimed that she needed to change the bulletin board in the narthex, since the season of Advent was almost upon them. But Charlotte could tell that she was hanging around after church to talk to her. She hadn't really expected Twila to be the one to bring it up, since Twila had the reputation for being quiet and nonconfrontational.

"Louise got a home health nurse for her

friend. Had you heard? And I think all of her family is coming in for the holiday weekend."

Charlotte nodded in response. Louise had called her last week to tell her the news.

"So will you be going home to be with your mother for Thanksgiving?" Twila was pulling out the thumbtacks and putting them in a cardboard box.

"Oh, I don't know. I usually like to work at the soup kitchen in Greensboro on Thanksgiving." Charlotte was taking off her stole. "And the wedding will be on Saturday of that weekend, so it doesn't do much good for me to be away." She pulled the front doors together and locked them.

"Oh yes, that wedding."

Charlotte heard it in her voice. "Yes," she said almost in a mocking voice, "that wedding." She threw away the extra bulletins, walked over to the display table, and checked the guest roster. She didn't say anything else. It was, after all, not her conversation.

"Reverend Stewart." Twila put down the tacks and borders and turned to Charlotte, who closed her eyes and thought, Here it comes!

"I have to ask, is it really prudent to have that wedding here?"

Charlotte cleared her throat. "Well, Mrs. Marks, both Wallace and Lana were baptized and confirmed here; their families are longtime members. I have been leading the two of them in counseling for several weeks and feel ready and clear about blessing this union. I think that covers all the bases for appropriate weddings here at Hope Springs." She continued. "I have read the constitution and bylaws of the church and find that this wedding is in line with rules and traditions, so I don't really see why it wouldn't be prudent to have this wedding here."

Twila could tell that this was a touchy subject for the young preacher. She began to waver in her decision to bring it up. She turned back to the bulletin board and climbed up the stepladder. "Well, you have to know that people are unhappy. Everybody's wondering why they can't just go to the courthouse or do it at Jessie's house or something. Why do they have to flaunt it in front of everyone's face?"

Charlotte was livid. Even she hadn't expected the depth of emotion that would be unleashed at the mention of this situation. Suddenly words were coming out of her mouth she hadn't anticipated, but she did not stop them. "Having their wedding at the church is flaunting their relationship? That is the most hypocritical, un-Christian, evil thing I have ever heard. Lana and Wallace are children from this community. They are the grandchildren of women you supposedly care about. And now, suddenly, when they choose to have a family together, choose to make a commitment to each other and to God and to the baby she's carrying, the church wants to hide them, ignore them, or, worse, cast them out?"

Twila didn't say anything for a few minutes. She had turned to face her now, and Charlotte really thought the conversation was over. She began walking to the door. But then Twila turned back around to talk to the wall. "I think the deacon board is going to have a meeting about this. Grady said so this morning. As chairman, he thinks they need to decide."

"And did you come to me as the representative of the chairman and the board of deacons?" Charlotte moved towards Twila.

"Well, not officially, I just told Grady that I would say something to you." She was still standing on the ladder, a few feet above Charlotte. She looked down at her.

"Then, Mrs. Marks, you go back and tell your husband, the chairman of the board of deacons, that we can have a meeting if he would like one, but these young people are faithful members of this church, and if I have to bring the sheriff to stand at the door and deal with the board of deacons, including your husband, the chairman, Wallace and Lana will be married here." Charlotte was a box, tight at the corners, opened on top.

Twila snapped her head around to face the empty board in front of her. Charlotte pulled open one of the swinging doors to the sanctuary and walked towards her office. She felt her face flush. As she got to the chancel she heard the phone ringing. She hurried back to answer it.

"Hope Springs Church," she said breathlessly on the fifth ring.

"Charlotte?" There was a pause. "I didn't know if I would reach you." It was her mother. "Are you okay? You sound all breathy or something."

Charlotte didn't say anything. It was like the

topping on a very bad day. She considered hanging up.

"Charlotte? Are you still there?"

"Yeah, I'm here. I ran from the sanctuary is all." She moved around the desk and sat down in her chair, her robe still on. "What do you want?"

"I'm your mother. Do I have to want something to call?" She said it very lightly, and Charlotte wondered if she had been drinking.

"Are you all right? Is everything okay?" Charlotte was sounding more like the mother now.

"Dear, I'm fine. I just wanted to talk to you, see how things are going at the church. I miss you is all."

"Are you back at Charter?"

There was a pause. "No. I haven't been back there in a long time. I've been sober almost two years now. I'm staying with the program, Charlotte. I told you that the last time I saw you."

Silence.

"The holidays are coming up. I thought maybe we could get together, have a meal or something." She waited for a response.

"Oh, I don't know. It's really busy here. And the holidays are the most busy time. I don't think it'll be possible." She hated this.

"What if I come to your house? I could cook us a Thanksgiving meal there."

"Thanks, Mom, but I'll be serving lunch at the shelter in town. Then I'll have to come back here and work on a wedding. It'll be a busy weekend for me."

"Oh." Her mother sounded wounded. "Okay, well, maybe Christmas then."

"Yeah, maybe Christmas."

"So how are things?" Her mother was not going to go away easily.

"Things are fine, Mother. It's Sunday. I'm tired. I just got through teaching Sunday School to a class of older men, most of whom were sleeping. Then I preached a sermon no one was interested in and just had a fight with the wife of the chairman of the board of deacons. Okay? I'm fine. Things are fine."

She heard the side door open and close. Twila must have finished what she was doing and left. She took a deep breath.

"Well, then I guess you'd like to get home and relax a little." Her mother's voice was hurt, full.

"Yeah. I have to go to the hospital later."

Charlotte was stretched and empty.

"Then we'll talk again."

Charlotte couldn't be sure if it was a question or statement.

"Yeah, we'll talk later. Take care now. Bye bye." She hung up the phone quickly. She sat back in her chair and put her hands on top of her head. She was still angry at the conversation in the narthex with Twila, still frustrated at the people in the church, and still struggling with years of ambivalence towards her mother.

She admitted to herself that she wasn't surprised by the response from the church to the wedding, but that didn't lessen the disappointment. How can I be their pastor knowing that they feel this way? she wondered. Then she slid her hands over her face, dropped her head, and thought about praying, but, deep down, she knew she didn't know how.

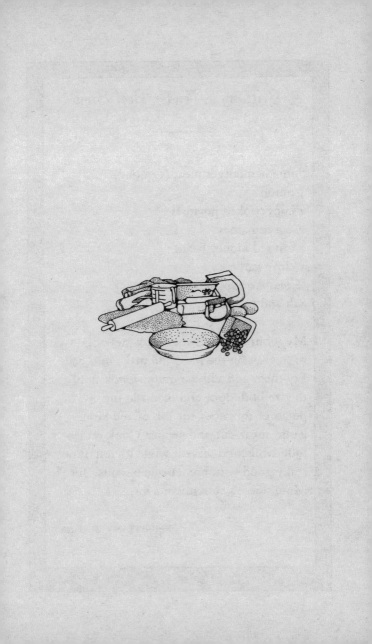

Brittany's Tender Beef Stew

Some hamburger meat (1 pound)
1 onion
4 cups cooked potatoes
1 can tomatoes
1 can red kidney beans
1 clove garlic
½ teaspoon sugar
Salt and pepper

My mom makes the best beef stew. She says to put salt on the meat and make into balls. Fry them and add the onion. Cook until they're both done and then add the potatoes, tomatoes, the can of red beans, garlic, sugar, salt, and pepper. Cook on low a little while, and serve it while it's hot. It's really good with homemade biscuits. But Mom doesn't cook them a lot.

—BRITTANY KLENNER

The Cookbook Committee decided to hold their November meeting at the church office since Louise now had a nursing assistant to stay with Roxie a few hours each day and Charlotte had a meeting later that morning with Nadine and Brittany.

It was Friday, a week before the wedding, and the air was brisk. The sky was thick with the anticipation of winter. For reasons of support and maintaining a source of strength, Jessie asked Margaret to serve as director of the small wedding planned for the Saturday of the Thanksgiving weekend. There would be a brief rehearsal on Friday evening, with a meal to follow in the Fellowship Hall. The service would be at 2:00 P.M., with a simple reception later at Jessie's house.

Since it was Charlotte's favorite time of year to be outside, she had taken a long walk around the church. When she got back to her office door, all four of the women were waiting for her. Jessie and Margaret were trying not to look nervous, but, in spite of their strong appearance, they worried about the wedding. Louise still had a frenzied look about her that everyone had come to expect, and Beatrice was busy pulling weeds from the flower bed by the steps.

"Wow! You're all early." Charlotte fumbled with her keys. "Everything okay?" She unlocked the door and led them to her office.

"Fine" was the mumbled response.

"Just great," replied Beatrice. They took seats around the pastor's desk. Beatrice pulled out a folder, and Margaret and Jessie handed her a few recipes they'd been asked to deliver.

"How's Ms. Roxie this week?" Charlotte hadn't been by to visit in a few days.

"She's better from her cold, but she's still got a bad cough. The nursing assistant comes by three times a week now and the nurse once. She stays in the bed more than she did a few weeks ago." Louise sat near the preacher's desk.

"Is her family still coming for the weekend?" Margaret had gotten a chair from the choir room and was setting it next to Louise.

"The children are." Louise paused. "George can't get away." She said this with a bit of sarcasm. "They're just coming for Thursday afternoon."

Charlotte said, "You've been mighty good to your friend, Ms. Fisher." They all nodded.

"Call me Louise, Charlotte, please."

Charlotte took off her coat. "Yes, ma'am, Louise."

Louise rolled her eyes.

"Do you need any help preparing the meal?" Beatrice was opening up her folder and putting her other things beside her chair.

"That'd be nice, Bea, but I don't think anybody is concerned about the meal. I thought I'd order one of those meals from the K&W. You can get everything for about five dollars a person." She looked at the other women with a sense of triumph at discovering such a bargain. "That includes the turkey, dressing, a few vegetables, and a pie. All I have to do is fix the tea."

Margaret chimed in. "You can probably get

that there too." She was really being facetious, but Louise seemed to think about the possibility and made a mental note.

Beatrice looked appalled. "Nonsense. You can't have Roxie's family coming from out of state and give them takeout food on Thanksgiving." She emphasized the words. "I'll help you fix a home-cooked meal. Robin's family are the only ones coming this year; so I'll just cook enough for you and your bunch too."

Margaret and Jessie raised their eyebrows at each other. Louise shrugged her shoulders. "Yes, ma'am." And she saluted Bea with a wave of her fingers from her brow while glancing over towards Charlotte.

"Well"—Beatrice was counting the recipes she had—"I guess what you all brought today gives us about half of what we need." She looked over the papers. "Anybody got any ideas about how to get some more?"

"Bea, I've called everybody I know. Lots of people have promised, but I've just not gotten any new ones." Jessie shrugged her shoulders.

"Same for me," said Margaret.

Louise didn't say anything. All the women sat thinking for a while.

"What about asking the children?" It was Charlotte who posed the question.

Beatrice looked up at her. "What do you mean?"

"I don't know for sure. But maybe in Sunday School we could ask the teachers to have each child tell their favorite thing to eat and then write down the recipe. They'd be simple, but it would give us a few more pages in the book and would involve the children."

Margaret and Jessie nodded. It seemed even Louise liked the idea.

Beatrice studied the notion for a few minutes. "I think that's a great thought, Charlotte. I'll work on that this week."

There was a break in the conversation while Beatrice wrote down the plan. It was Charlotte who asked, "So what else is going on with you ladies? Mrs. Jenkins, are you getting ready for next week?" The minister sat back in her chair.

Jessie shifted in her seat and looked at Margaret. "It's Jessie, dear, and I'm not sure." Then she added, "Maybe this isn't a good idea."

All of the women were surprised at her response.

"Of course it's a good idea," said Margaret.

"It's going to be a beautiful day in the life of Hope Springs Church." She was trying to sound excited.

Beatrice closed her folder. "Margaret, maybe Jessie's right. This is a big deal in the community."

Margaret was preparing for a fight. She sat up in her seat.

"No, Margaret, Bea's right. It is a big deal." Jessie appeared defeated.

"So, it's a big deal. It is what the church is supposed to be about. And if it's a big deal, then we've made it a big deal. There is no reason we shouldn't have events like this all the time." She looked over at the preacher, who was nodding in agreement.

Beatrice added quickly, "That's great for a white person to say, but we don't know what it's like for Jessie."

Louise turned to face her. Beatrice was constantly surprising her.

"I don't know what you mean, Bea. Jessie's fine. Nothing's going to happen to her. What do you think, the KKK's going to come burn a cross in her yard?"

"Margaret, it does still happen." This was Louise.

"Oh, that's nonsense." Margaret turned to Jessie for confirmation.

Jessie hesitated in the hope that someone else would speak, but no one responded. They waited to hear from her. She shifted in her seat before she began. Slowly she spoke what had been on her heart for some time. "No, they're right. I don't know what to expect." She sat back.

"But it isn't me I'm worried about. Lord, I'm too old to be whipped. But I worry about Wallace. He already had huge boulders in his way being black and poor. But marrying a white girl, having a mixed baby." She shook her head. "White people think we want our boys to marry light, but this isn't welcomed by either race." She looked around at the women. "It's going to be a hard life for him."

She paused and took a tissue from her purse. "And you really don't know, Margaret. None of you really know." She focused her attention on Margaret. "Cruelty and meanness haven't gone away just because we're able to eat at the same table or go to church together. It's alive and well in this community, this state, this country. It's just a little veiled is all. But it's still alive and thriving. And young Wallace and Lana have been protected from it for the most part."

She dabbed the tissue under her eyes and continued. "In some ways I think it's even worse for our young people. At least we knew our enemies when I was young. They were loud and straightforward. Nowadays, they're not always so recognizable. So that you begin to think it's you, that something's wrong with you. That you're imagining things or just being paranoid. We've been brainwashed to believe that it can't be racism; that's been outlawed and forgotten. We like to think it's ancient history." She stopped again.

"Only it isn't so ancient." She dropped the tissue in her lap. "And you can't outlaw the way a person feels. You can't punish what's in a person's heart. And no matter how many laws have been passed, everybody knows that when a black person is walking up to white folks, that's what they see first, a black person, the dark color of their skin."

Friendship Cake

The women were silent while Jessie put her head down and folded her hands across her lap.

Instead of Beatrice, Margaret spoke this time. "I'm sorry."

"So, what can we do, Jess?" Louise was asking.

"Lou, you got your hands full as it is." Jessie sat up. She took in a breath and looked at Charlotte. She was nervous but resolved.

"We're going to have a wedding, and we're going to try and act happy for these two young people. And I tell you now, up front, I appreciate what you're doing for me and my family. Margaret, for directing, Preacher, for doing the service and for apparently having quite a fuss with Twila."

Charlotte surveyed the women's faces, wondering how that news had gotten around.

"And Beatrice and Louise, for handling the reception."

Louise seemed surprised. She turned to Beatrice with a questioning look.

"Oh, I forgot to tell you, Lou. But it won't be a lot of trouble, and Roxie can come too. It'll do her good to get out. Dick said we can borrow a wheelchair from the funeral home."

205

Louise rolled her eyes and laughed. Margaret and Charlotte smiled.

"Your friendship means a lot, and I thank you." Jessie looked at all of the women.

After a few moments of quiet appreciation, Margaret spoke up. "Um, speaking of Dick, Beatrice, I understand the two of you were at the Western Sizzlin' Steak House last Friday night." Margaret grinned while Beatrice opened the folder back up and began to shuffle the papers.

"Why, Margaret, you wouldn't be spreading gossip now, would you?" Louise was speaking now.

Suddenly, Beatrice had a look of great pleasure. Finally the tables were turned. "Why, Margaret! I'm surprised at you!"

Margaret crossed her legs. "Now, I never claimed to have a problem with *happy* meddlesome gossip." She accented the word *happy*.

The women laughed. "And it is happy, isn't it, Bea?"

Beatrice's face reddened. "Well, it's certainly meddlesome." She never responded to the implied question about her and Dick's relationship.

Louise was about to push her when Nadine knocked on the office door. "Am I too early?"

Charlotte got up from her desk. "No, no, come in. We were just discussing"——she paused while Beatrice looked at her with a certain amount of trepidation——"the cookbook."

Nadine walked in. "Oh yeah, I heard about the cookbook. I wish I had something to offer, but I'm afraid I'm not much of a cook." She had Brittany by the hand.

"Well, actually the preacher had a great idea that maybe the children would like to give some recipes." Beatrice leaned towards Brittany from her seat. "What's your favorite thing to eat, young lady?"

Brittany reached behind her mother and stood with her face at the back of her legs.

"Oh, you're not shy. Come stand around here, Brittany. Tell them what you like to eat." The little girl peeked from around Nadine's legs at Beatrice.

"I like beef stew," she mumbled. And she hid her face again.

"Is that right? I like beef stew too." This was Margaret.

"Can you remember what you put in it, Nadine? If so, we could get a recipe right here." Beatrice pulled out a piece of paper.

"Um, sure," Nadine said. And with Brittany stuck to the back of her legs, she walked over to Charlotte's desk and wrote the ingredients.

"Great!" said Charlotte. "Brittany and I can write the instructions together, can't we?" Brittany looked around and smiled at Charlotte.

While Nadine was writing, the other women began to fold up the chairs and prepare to leave.

"We'll see everyone this weekend." Beatrice was following Louise, who had slipped out first. "Lou, we need to talk about the reception."

Margaret and Jessie walked out together, saying their good-byes. Charlotte waved but stayed at her desk while Brittany came around and sat in her lap.

"There, that's what I can remember. And you cook the meat and onions first and then add the other stuff. I usually let it simmer about ten minutes before I serve it. But it's pretty good. Some people like it hot, but Brittany doesn't like hot sauce, do you, honey?"

Brittany turned up her nose, jumped out of Charlotte's lap, and went over to the shelf where there were toys for the children who came to the office. She picked up a windup monkey.

"Is she okay to mess with that stuff?" Nadine was standing beside Charlotte at the desk.

"Oh sure, it's fine."

"Well, then, I'm going to run. Remember to ask the preacher your questions about heaven, okay, baby?" She went over and smoothed her daughter's hair.

"I'll just be an hour or so." Then she wound up the toy for Brittany and looked back at Charlotte. "I really thank you, Pastor. I never had a preacher that I could leave my daughter with. Brittany really likes you." She kissed Brittany on the cheek and walked out. The door closed behind her.

"Well, there goes my speech to your mother about baby-sitting!" Charlotte said this as Brittany looked at her somewhat confused.

"So, you want to tell me about this beef stew?"

Brittany pulled the other toys onto the floor. "It's tender," she said.

Charlotte wrote down the heading "Tender Beef Stew." Then she rewrote the list of ingredients that Nadine had given her. "What can you tell me about how your mother makes Tender Beef Stew?"

"She makes balls and fries them. That's the best part."

Charlotte wrote down what the little girl said.

"Then she mixes everything together." She was playing with a baby doll that had been left in the hallway the previous Sunday. "And it's really good with homemade biscuits, but Mom doesn't cook them a lot."

Charlotte smiled and wrote down her words exactly as she said them. She thought it would be funny for the cookbook. "So tell me what you want to know about heaven." Charlotte was curious if this was a real concern or something just manufactured by Nadine.

"Is it nice?" Brittany asked.

"Oh, it's real nice," Charlotte responded, thinking this was pretty easy.

"Are there dogs in heaven?"

"I don't know. Do you like dogs?"

"I've got one named Teddy. I like to play with him."

"Then dogs will be in heaven too. The nice ones, like Teddy."

"Do you know anybody in heaven?" Brittany had put the monkey with the baby doll. It appeared as if she was pairing up the toys.

"I have a sister in heaven." Charlotte stopped writing and watched the little girl playing with the toys. "And of course Jesus is there."

"Do you ever get to come back when you go to heaven?"

"I'm not sure. I think you're so happy when you're there that you don't want to come back." Charlotte began putting books back on the shelves.

"Does your sister come back?"

Suddenly, the questions were harder. Charlotte sat down on the floor with Brittany. "No, I don't think so. But sometimes I feel her near me. She was a very funny girl." She picked up a stuffed toy and rubbed Brittany's ear with its tail.

"I'm a funny girl too." Brittany reached for the dog and rubbed Charlotte's ear.

"Yes, you are a funny girl too."

"When I go to heaven, I'll come back and tell you what your sister's doing."

Charlotte began to fix the baby doll's dress. "That would be very nice of you."

They played with the toys; then Brittany colored a few pictures while Charlotte worked on the wedding bulletin.

"Can I come to the wedding?" Brittany asked.

"Yes, you may," Charlotte replied. "Have you ever been to a wedding?"

Brittany began to think. "I went to my aunt's wedding. She got married in a park. It was real hot." She searched for a red crayon. "I'm going to marry Stephen Mitchell. He has a swimming pool." She said this as she looked for another picture to color.

"You are?" Charlotte asked. "And when are you planning to get married?"

"Oh, at least not until I'm thirteen."

"Well, I'm sure your mother will be happy about that." Charlotte laughed to herself.

"What about you? Are you married?"

"Nope." Charlotte began to type the bulletin. "But Stephen Mitchell sounds like a pretty great guy; maybe I'll marry him before you do." Charlotte was teasing the little girl.

"That would be okay. Then when you're finished being married to him, I'll marry him." Brittany seemed to have an answer for everything. She pulled out a picture she had colored and handed it to Charlotte. "This is for you."

Charlotte took the picture. "Oh! It's so beautiful. I'm going to hang it up on the wall." And she took a piece of tape and taped it to the wall behind her chair. Brittany watched proudly.

"You want to play the organ while I print the bulletin?"

Brittany nodded, scooped up a toy, and ran through the office door to the nursery down the hall. It was only a few minutes until Charlotte heard the motor of the organ start up and Brittany begin to play.

Charlotte thought about the little girl's questions, the ideas of heaven, the notion of whether one could ever come back. She had never really considered if Serena would make a choice to return, if such a choice were possible. She wondered how it might be to see her sister back from death and resurrection.

Would she finally be whole, or would there always be hidden pieces, which she would spend eternity trying to uncover? Missing parts that kept her life and death an unsolved puzzle?

Had she been loosed from her previous binding life, or were there ropes still tied around her hopes and dreams? Was she young, or had the years of reflection on what had taken place and what had not taken place aged her in some way that made her different, unrecognizable?

Charlotte rarely allowed herself the opportunity to think about Serena, her life, her death, her whereabouts. Pondering the past created an emotional and mental spinning that, as a rule, Charlotte chose to deny. It was, in her mind, a futile line of thinking. A process without a product. A task without a plan. A sinking, dropping, falling journey that could lead her nowhere.

When she realized that she had stepped back into a place she generally refused to go, she looked up, and Brittany, having grown bored with the organ, was standing in the doorway of Charlotte's office.

"Hey!" Charlotte was startled. She pulled the bulletin from the printer, dropped it on her desk, and asked, "How about we take a walk before your mother gets back?"

Brittany nodded, and Charlotte moved around the desk and headed towards the door.

"And here," she said, as she walked back from where the toys had been and grabbed the little stuffed dog they had been playing with, "you can have this. It can be a Thanksgiving gift from me."

Brittany seemed pleased, but then she stopped. "You don't give gifts for Thanksgiving," she said. "You give gifts at Christmas." She looked confused.

"Well, you can give gifts whenever you like," the preacher responded. "And besides, you gave me a gift of the picture. So I give you this little dog as a gift back to you."

Brittany thought about this a minute, then said, "Thanksgiving must be a good time to give gifts."

"Why's that?" Charlotte asked.

"Because then you're really thankful." And she took the dog and gave it a hug.

Charlotte laughed and held the little girl's hand as they walked through the cemetery and around the outside of the sanctuary, down the road to the parsonage, and then back to the church. As they got back to the driveway, Nadine was pulling up.

She rolled down the window. "What are you two doing?"

"We went for a walk, Mommy. And Charlotte gave me this little dog for a Thanksgiving present." She dropped Charlotte's hand and ran to her mother's door.

"How sweet of her. What a great puppy; he looks like Teddy."

Charlotte walked around to the driver's side. "I hope everything's fine." She noticed the groceries in the backseat.

"Oh yeah." Nadine looked back at Brittany. "Did you have a good talk?"

Brittany was playing with the dog along the side of the car. "Yep. We talked about heaven. Charlotte's sister is there."

Nadine looked at Charlotte, who smiled and nodded.

"Yes. Brittany had some very good questions."

Nadine was a little surprised. "Oh?" she said.

Brittany nodded and looked up at the preacher. "And I told her all about the beef stew."

"Yes. It will be a very special recipe in our cookbook." Charlotte rubbed Brittany's back. "Well, give me a hug before you go. Did you leave anything in my office?"

Brittany hugged Charlotte and shook her head no.

"Thank you, Pastor." Nadine was watching as Brittany moved around the front of the car.

Charlotte went around and opened the passenger's side door.

"Please call me Charlotte. Brittany does." And she waved at the little girl and her mother through the window.

"Bye, bye now!"

Nadine and Brittany both waved good-bye, and Charlotte went back into her office. She pulled the door shut and locked it. She sat down at her desk and was glancing over the bulletin when the sudden crash of metal and glass splintered the air.

Charlotte ran from the office and saw that Nadine's car had been hit by a large truck as she was backing out of the church driveway. Right away, the moments broke off in pieces, jagged and sharp. Charlotte was a blur of spectator and participant in a tragedy that was unfolding before her eyes.

She found her way to the driver's side of the car. Nadine was bleeding from her nose, but she was conscious, moving her hands, trying to undo her seat belt.

"Brittany?" she screamed. "Where's Brittany?"

Charlotte looked around frantically. It seemed time sped up and slowed down in the same moment. The truck had crushed the right side of the automobile; the passenger's side door was forced open by the impact. Brittany hadn't had time to put on her seat belt and had been thrown from the car. Charlotte looked on the side opposite Nadine. The child's body was in a parking lot, forty feet away from the stopped car. She ran to Brittany before Nadine could get free.

The little girl was dead. It was obvious from the vast amount of blood, and the way she lay, her neck broken from the impact. Charlotte swept the body into her arms and began to scream to the men in the truck, who sat paralyzed. "Go get some help! Go call an ambulance!"

A man jumped out of the truck, the passenger's side, and ran to the church office. The driver, dazed, got out and went to Nadine, who was still struggling to get to her daughter. "Brittany! I want to see Brittany!"

Charlotte was crying and holding the little

girl. She watched as the earth split itself from the sky, the piece of time and matter of which she was a part float into space.

Finally, Nadine was freed from the wreckage, and Charlotte saw her running towards them, bloody and broken.

"Oh, God. No. Please no . . ." Nadine did not even feel the pain of her injuries. Only this. Only the torment of seeing this death. Charlotte gave her the body and held them both. Time stopped while the shard of torn life whirled out of control. The screams grew louder than the approaching sirens.

"My baby! Oh, God, no, not my baby!"

Charlotte held them tighter as the mother rocked her dead child. Then suddenly Nadine stopped. She focused on Charlotte with a wild, desperate look. "Do something!" she cried. "Here, take her, do something!" And she handed the dead body to Charlotte.

Charlotte fought the mother. Tears streamed down her face; words choked in her throat. "Nadine, I can't do anything . . . I can't . . ." And she struggled with Nadine to give the child back.

The ambulance attendants ran to the two women. They reached out for the little girl, trying to take her from Nadine. She screamed at them, a madwoman, *"No!"* She looked back at Charlotte, fierce and loosed. "Make her come back! You make her come back!"

Charlotte, only a wisp of life herself, took Brittany's body in her arms, and, for a suspended second, an eternal pause in the course of events, it seemed something was sewing her tattered shreds of faith together like a web of healing. Tighter and tighter it seemed to wrap around her heart. And suddenly she felt strong and rooted, magnificent and tall. She was a tree, growing straight into the heart of God.

Maybe, she thought in that blast of temptation, just maybe. Maybe it could be so. Maybe God was saving up all of the grace I never felt until now. For this detail. This time. This place. Maybe something, somebody will come, just for this moment. For this child. For this mother. For me. And even though the thought never formed words that anyone heard, it rumbled in her mind like thunder.

She prayed with every cell and fiber within her. It was a whisper, a scream, a prayer beyond the borders of despair. "O God, please."

But like a storm of wind that yanks and pulls

everything into its funneled mouth, the prayer
sucked her hope dry and left its remains scattered across the pavement. The web of faith
pulled apart. The tree snapped in the wind, and
the little girl did not breathe again.

One EMT took Brittany from Charlotte's
aching arms while the other helped Nadine
onto a stretcher. Charlotte stayed there on the
ground, without moving, until all of the ambu-
lances, fire trucks, and curious bystanders had
driven away.

Lots of people came and tried to console her,
but she would not move. She would not be lifted
from where she had prayed and been turned
down.

BEATRICE HAD GONE into the office. Jessie and
Margaret were sitting beside Charlotte. Louise
was leaning against the wall of the church. It had
been hours since the accident.

Everyone was relieved when Charlotte's
mother, Joyce, drove up. She parked near Louise
and Beatrice, talked briefly with them, then
walked over to the three women sitting in the
parking lot. Charlotte had blood smeared all

over her. Jessie and Margaret got up, shook their heads towards Joyce, and left the mother and daughter alone.

Joyce sat down beside Charlotte but didn't say anything. She watched as the others, friends of her daughter, went into the church. She knew they were there if she needed them. She picked up a pebble and rolled it around in her hand.

Day turned to evening. Light faded, and still the two women sat in silence. Finally, as the sun dropped low and darkness hid their faces from each other, her mother spoke. "I'm going to have a cigarette if it's all right."

Charlotte said nothing while her mother pulled out a pack of cigarettes and lit one. She took a long, slow drag and fanned the smoke away from her daughter.

"These are Serena's brand. Menthol," she said with a sigh. "I used to hate menthol. It always felt like I was smoking a Tic Tac."

Still nothing from Charlotte, who sat with her legs bent, her hands empty in her lap, her head dropped.

"I found a pack in her room after she died." She took another drag. "I think it was the only thing you didn't clean out." She tapped at the tip of the cigarette to release the ashes. "It's all I smoke now."

A car went past. It slowed down while the passengers looked out the window at the two women sitting in the parking lot in the dark. Joyce waved them away.

There was another long, empty pause.

"You know, we had an argument before she went off and took all those drugs." Joyce let the smoke fill her lungs. "It was about you."

Charlotte moved for the first time. She didn't look up, but she shifted her legs from one side to the other.

"She said I drove you away with my drinking. That if I wasn't a drunk, you would have stayed at home instead of going to graduate school. She said I pulled the two of you apart. That since you had gone, you never called her anymore or tried to see her." Joyce ran her hands across her arms. "She was terrible that night, loud and angry and so full of bitterness and rage. I had never seen her like that." Joyce crushed the cigarette by her side.

A car horn blew in the distance, and a flurry of bats flew overhead.

"She wanted to come and see me over the

weekend." Charlotte spoke with her head down. "I said no." She stopped. "I said that I was too busy or had a class or work. I don't know what I said. But it was the only time I said no to her." Her voice trailed off. "So she killed herself."

Joyce sat up. Someone was turning on lights in the church's Fellowship Hall.

"You think Serena killed herself because she couldn't go to see you for the weekend?" Joyce dropped the pack of cigarettes that were in her lap and took Charlotte's chin in her hand. She lifted her daughter's face so that they were eye to eye. "That's what you think? You made Serena commit suicide because you turned her down, once?"

Charlotte's eyes filled with tears.

"Oh, child." Joyce felt her heart explode. "Child, my sweet Charlotte, child." She reached out and hugged her daughter. "Serena got mad and took too many drugs. She was mad at everybody. Serena had been mad, out of control, for a long time. You knew that, didn't you?"

Charlotte did not respond.

"I was a terrible mother to her, to both of you, and I'll have to live with that for the rest of my life. But you, you've done nothing wrong.

You were a wonderful sister to Serena. You were the mother to her that I wasn't. If anyone's to blame for her death, it's me, not you. You did nothing wrong. Nothing." Joyce pulled away and looked at Charlotte again.

They were both crying now.

After a while Charlotte spoke. "Then why doesn't God hear my prayers?" she asked through the tears. "If I'm so good, Mama, why doesn't he hear my prayers? Why did he let Serena die?" she shouted. "Why did he let this little baby girl die? Why doesn't he hear me when I pray?" Charlotte sobbed and fell on her mother's shoulders.

It seemed like a long time before the older woman spoke.

"I don't know, child. I have wondered the same thing so many times." Joyce smoothed back her daughter's hair. "Every time I drove by the liquor store or tried not to reach for the bottle, I would pray. I put pictures of you and Serena all around the house, and I would pray, 'Help me not to drink, God. Help me to be a good mother to my daughters.' But then a bill would come due or I would make a mistake with one of you, and I felt nothing but the taste of vodka calling me." She wiped a tear from Charlotte's cheek.

"But, deep down, I think God always heard me. Even though I wasn't good, I think God hears me." She pulled Charlotte towards her. "And I know that God hears you when you pray. I know that."

Another car went by and slowed down but then kept going.

"I think it's just that sometimes we want an answer from God that he can't give. And because we're so sure of what we want the answer to be, we can't receive the one he gives us."

Charlotte began to cry again. Joyce reached in her pocket for a tissue.

"And, Charlotte, some of your anger at God isn't about God at all. The choices I made, the choices your father made, even and especially the choice that Serena made, were our choices. And we hurt you because of our choices. But God didn't do that, we did. And before you can forgive us, like I know you think you have, you've got to be mad at us first. And I would rather you be mad and yell and scream at me, than be so distant, so far away, so unreachable."

Friendship Cake

She pulled her daughter to her. "I love you, Charlotte, and I am so sorry."

Charlotte crawled into her mother's lap and stayed there, her mother rocking her, until they heard the door of the church open and close.

A few minutes passed, and Joyce finally spoke again. "Are you okay to go in now?"

Joyce felt her daughter nod her head against her neck. She waited a few minutes and added, "Well, you're a little big to carry."

Charlotte let out a quiet laugh, moved off her mother's lap, and picked herself up from the ground. Joyce got up too, and together they walked from the parking lot to the church.

Charlotte climbed in her mother's car. Joyce went in and spoke to the women still there, then came back out and drove her daughter home.

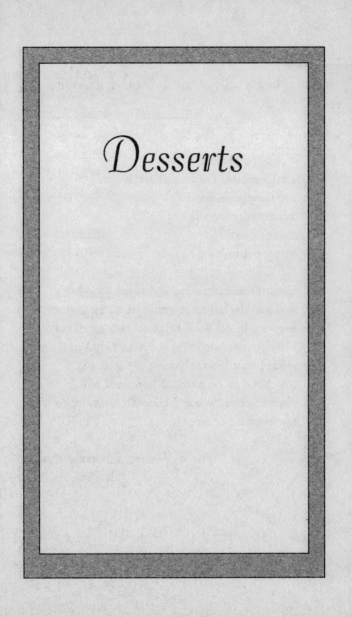

Desserts

Dick's Mexican Wedding Cookies

---

1 cup margarine
4 tablespoons confectioners' sugar
1½ teaspoons water
2 teaspoons vanilla
2 cups flour
1 cup pecans

Cream the margarine and sugar together
and add the other ingredients in the order
they are listed. Roll mixture into small balls.
Put these on a cookie sheet and chill in the
refrigerator before baking. Bake at 325°F
for about 12 minutes. When cool, roll in
confectioners' sugar. Makes about 5 dozen if
made small.

—DICK WITHERSPOON

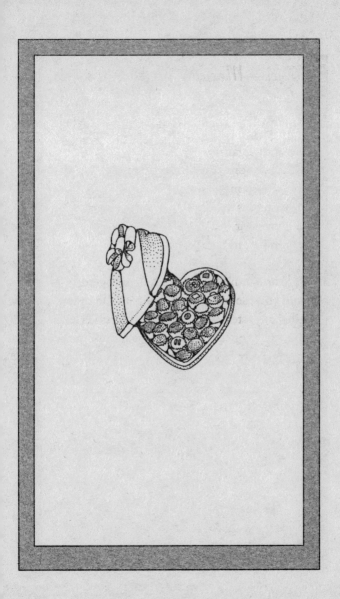

*T*he wedding was postponed because of the funeral and the overall disposition of the Hope Springs community. Brittany's death was a dark, heavy cloud that situated itself directly above the church and clung to the heads and hearts of those who attended.

Some people wanted to talk about death and issues of fear and mortality. Others climbed into their hard shells and spoke of the things that troubled them only in their faraway glances or in bowed shoulders and trembling hands. People began to accept the fact that expressions of grief are as individualized as tastes in music and preferences for how to hear bad news. Some want to be eased into the information or sounds, and others want it hard and fast.

Charlotte visited all the homes of the children who knew Brittany and let them ask her anything they wanted. It was a grueling and tiresome activity, but Charlotte was convinced that pastoral care sometimes means coloring pictures and watching cartoons until a child might finally be ready to ask if what happened to Brittany was also going to happen to her.

Somehow, in the midst of this haunting tragedy, Charlotte grew wings. She was certainly not at peace with what had happened, nor did she become unattached or unfeeling. She wasn't locked into her own displaced or aggravated grief. Rather, a foreign and intangible sense of calm took her over; it could best be described as being comfortable in the uncomfortable, digesting the fact that she was unable to fix everything. And now, because she understood this deeply and solidly within herself, she was actually capable of being still.

The funeral itself was simple and fitting for a child. It was straight to the point of celebrating a young and beautiful life, and clear in stating the fact that everyone who suffered in this loss desperately needed the presence and attention of God and the support and love of one another. Charlotte made no attempt to remove anyone's pain or gloss over the undeniable suffering of everyone involved.

Following Brittany's death the worship services were short and unassuming. There was no order of service printed in the bulletin. Only the Scripture reading for the day and the words of the Lord's Prayer were included, so that those who found themselves suddenly unable to remember anything would have the words in front of them. When she preached, for a couple of Sundays there was no sermon like before. She preached from the Psalms and openly discussed the terror of emptiness and the agony of searching for God.

She made no attempts to theologize or sermonize away the death of a child, and her prayers were barely audible. If she felt the need to change the order of the service, she did. If she sensed that they had sung enough verses, she stopped the hymn. If she suddenly felt the need to go down and kneel by the altar before she spoke, she walked down in the silence and awkwardness of the congregation and prayed. Nothing became important for the young preacher anymore except that she listen to her heart.

For the first time in her life, Charlotte considered herself among the ranks of the walking wounded, and, as for a recovering alcoholic, success for her was merely having made it through one day, one hour without having become victimized by her woundedness.

Much to everyone's surprise, the congregation responded positively to the changes. They began to appreciate the newfound freedom in the worship services, and they followed their leader's example. Sometimes one or two would not stand and sing while the others did. Often during the service someone from the congregation would just go to the front, kneel and pray, and then go back to her seat. Once an older gentleman interrupted the preacher and asked if he might read the Scripture because he needed to say the words out loud.

Something was being untied, untangled for the Hope Springs Community Church, but Charlotte was not interested in naming or diagnosing it. As she had the untimely death of a child, she just let it be.

She agreed that postponing the wedding for a few weeks was probably a good idea. At least there would be a little time to sit with the loss before trying to celebrate the happiness and goodwill of a wedding. Wallace and Lana and their families met with Charlotte and decided to put it off until the week before Christmas. They thought that would be better for the bride and groom anyway; they would have the few weeks off from school for the holidays to get moved into Jessie's house.

Janice rented the young couple an apartment in town, but after a few days of talking it over, Lana and Wallace decided that they would rather stay in the community near school and family. So Janice took the apartment, and Jessie invited her grandson and his soon-to-be wife to live with her. "Besides," she told them, "it'll be like having a built-in nanny."

The night before the wedding, right after the rehearsal, a snowstorm hit the Southeast, freezing the ground and roads and bringing to a halt driving, working, holiday shopping, and general day-to-day activities. Everything was stopped or silenced, everything, that is, except a wedding. Lana was convinced that a second postponement would mean cancellation. So, in spite of Lana's mother's pleas to wait until the following week, Charlotte agreed with the bride and kept the event as planned.

"I guess I'll need to clear off the parking lot and sidewalks." Charlotte was talking to Jessie on the phone that morning to tell her Lana's decision.

"You can't do all that by yourself. Wallace has gone to clean off the Wests' driveway, so I'm not sure how long he'll be. But I'll come after I finish baking."

"I could call some of the men from the church." Charlotte waited, but there was no response from Jessie.

Finally, she replied. "I expect that would render little to no results. I'll come as soon as I can, and we'll do what we can do and not worry about the rest." She stretched the phone cord to check on her cookies. "I'll see you a little later then."

"Yes. Bye now." And Charlotte hung up the phone. She knew the possibilities were slim that anybody would be enthusiastic about shoveling snow out of the church parking lot for a wedding they all opposed, but she still sat at her kitchen table trying to think of people who might be willing to put their prejudices aside and assist with the carrying out of this wedding. She could think of no one.

I could, she thought, call Grady and demand that the deacons handle this. But ordering their cooperation and assistance felt like making choices for the church leaders that they needed to make for themselves. So she decided that she would start shoveling in the morning and hope to have at least one path to the sanctuary and a few parking places cleared by the afternoon.

She dressed in her warmest clothes, found a shovel in the shed behind the parsonage, and trudged to the church to begin the burdensome task. She worked for what seemed an hour, a lone woman trying to make a path from the church to the road. Her vision became a blur of white and blue. Snow to sky and sky to snow, she pushed and pulled the shovel across the sidewalk and over her head. With her arms and fingers stiff from the exercise and numb from the cold, she dropped the shovel at her feet and sat down on the frozen porch to see how little she had accomplished.

The futility of her work made her laugh as she became aware of how similar it was to her progress as a minister. "Guess I haven't gotten very far, huh, God?"

Suddenly a voice responded. "You praying

Lynne Hinton

out here because you're locked out or are you one of those folks who thinks you're closer to God outside?"

The voice frightened Charlotte, and she turned around to find Grady Marks standing at her back. He had walked up from behind the church. "Twila figured you'd be out here by yourself; she sent you some coffee." And he handed her a thermos and a mug.

"Thanks. I didn't think to bring anything warm to drink, and it's pretty cold." She pulled her scarf back over her ears, took the thermos, and poured herself a cup of coffee. She screwed the top back on and handed it to the man now standing at her side. He waved it away, and she set it down beside her on the step. It was the medicine her cold limbs needed.

"Guess the wedding is still on then?"

Charlotte wasn't sure of the meaning of the question, whether or not there was more than one, so she merely nodded her head affirmatively.

"I suppose you know my thoughts about this."

Charlotte took a sip and shrugged her shoul-

240

ders. "I suppose I know your wife's interpretation of your thoughts about this."

Grady made fists with both of his hands and blew air into them, trying to get them warm. "A white girl and a black boy, it just don't seem natural to me."

Charlotte didn't look at Grady.

"But I tell you the truth, not much does seem natural anymore." He looked over at Charlotte, who was staring into her coffee. "A woman preacher. A little girl dying in the church parking lot. A big storm like this so early in the winter. Louise Fisher and that woman she's taking care of." He kicked his heel on the side of the porch. "I'm not sure I know what 'natural' is."

Charlotte simply nodded and smiled. She didn't feel defensive at being compared to a tragedy or a freak of nature like a snowstorm. She simply realized that this middle-aged white man was doing the best he could to articulate his discomfort with change and people who were unlike himself.

"Jessie's been a member of this church longer than I have. She taught my children the books of the Bible and came over to my house to pray with me when my mama passed. I have a lot of respect for her." He looked towards the back of the church, where his truck was parked. "So what I'm trying to say is that I've come to help you clean off the lot and get ready for this afternoon. A couple others said they'd come by too, so if you've got other things that you need to do, we'll take care of this."

Charlotte lifted her head as three farm trucks came up the road and turned into the driveway of the church. Six or seven men got out, reached for shovel picks, and started to spread out across the frozen lot and make a way.

It was the picture of grace, undeniable, indescribable grace, and Charlotte wanted to laugh and cry at the same time. It was the quenching of an old and tired thirst. And the moment was sweet, so very, very sweet that she wrapped herself in the vision of it all and drank it in like the steaming hot coffee.

The men, all members of the church, deacons and teachers, choir members and lay leaders, labored all morning, shoveling and raking, until the area was free from snow and ice and there was no hindrance for the wedding.

Charlotte was throwing salt on the sidewalk when she saw one lone, brown Chevrolet drive past with out-of-state plates. The black man stopped, looked out the window at the men and one woman who had been shoveling snow at the church, shook his head, and drove on.

JESSIE WAS PUTTING on her gloves as she walked through the back door and straight into the arms of her ex-husband as he stood on the porch getting ready to knock. She was so shocked at the presence of somebody standing where she hadn't expected anyone that she didn't even realize who it was until she had fallen back into the storage freezer that stood in the corner of the screened-in porch.

"Jesus Almighty!" she said as she put her hand across her heart.

"No. Just James." He smiled a wide-toothed grin and stepped inside. "You all right?"

Jessie picked up her right glove, which had fallen from her hands, and began smoothing down the front of her coat. "I'm fine. You just shouldn't go sneaking up on people."

They stood awkwardly on the porch until James finally asked, "Can I come in a few minutes?"

Jessie looked beyond him towards the road. "I really need to go and help the preacher scrape off the sidewalks before the ceremony. There's just the two of us to do it." She looked at James, studied him. It had been a few years since she'd seen him. He still looks the same, she thought.

"I don't think they need you."

Jessie was surprised. "They? What do you mean?"

James took off his hat and held it by his side. "You still going to that white church on the corner?"

Jessie nodded.

"Well, I just drove by there, and they've cleaned off the whole lot, the porch, and the sidewalks. I thought there must be some other event for all that work on such a cold day."

"Who's they?" Jessie moved closer to the door and tried to see down the street to the church.

"I don't know, but it looked like about four trucks, eight or ten white men. They were almost through by the time I drove by." He brushed the snow from the shoulders of his coat.

"Oh." This was all Jessie could say.

A few minutes passed. James cleared his throat.

"Oh," she said again, looking over at James. "Yeah, sure, come on in." She looked at her watch and began taking off her coat and boots. She reached for James's coat and hat, and he handed them both to her. He walked inside and looked around.

"Things look the same, Jess." He went over to the mantel and began looking at the pictures. Then he lifted his nose in the air. "Baking a pie?" And he smiled.

"No, just a few cookies for the reception. A couple of the women from the church are hosting it, but I felt like they could use a little help." Jessie went into the kitchen. "I still have some coffee from breakfast. I could heat us up a cup in the microwave."

James nodded. "Yeah, that sounds good." He continued to look at the pictures of his family while Jessie fixed the coffee.

"Sugar?" she asked.

"Yes, babe?" He answered in the teasing manner he always did and walked to the kitchen.

Jessie smiled and shook her head. She put a teaspoon of sugar in a cup of coffee and handed it to him.

He took it and winked a thank-you.

"Janice call you?" Jessie was curious about how he found out.

"Yeah, last week." He put the cup down on the counter. "I thought I'd surprise you."

Jessie took a sip from her cup, walked to the den, and said, "Well, you certainly did that!" She had a seat on the sofa.

James followed and sat across from her in the recliner. "So, little Wallace got a white girl pregnant and they're all going to live with you?" He blew across his cup trying to cool the coffee.

"Yes. I suppose that sums up the situation."

"Hmm. You still working?"

"Only part-time these days. I'll probably completely retire though when the baby's born. I want these two to finish school."

James took a sip.

"You still in Washington?" Jessie crossed her legs and pulled at her heavy wool sweater. She wondered how long he was planning to stay.

"Yeah, still in the nation's capital, working at the bank as a security guard. Been there seventeen years, only robbed once." He grinned at Jessie.

"You're too old to be a security guard." She was teasing him now.

"I figure the older you are, the less likely they are to shoot you." He set his cup on the table beside him and folded his hands in his lap. He saw Jessie look at the clock on the wall. He shifted in his chair and suddenly appeared serious.

"Janice says I can stay with her in her new apartment, but I don't want to make things worse for you." He rubbed his legs. "I'll not stay, if it's a problem." He looked over at Jessie for the answer.

She waited for a minute. She liked having him vulnerable like this. She enjoyed the softness of his temper, the polite way he would ask for her permission on such occasions. She savored the tenderness of it. "Of course, you'll stay," she said, waving her hand. "Wallace would love to have you here, and the family could use your support. Besides," she said, "I've got two of your favorite pies in the fridge."

James lifted an eyebrow.

"James Junior likes them too." Jessie said this to dismiss any idea James might have that she had been hoping he would come. She cut her eyes at the only man she'd ever loved and let the expectant air fill her chest.

James nodded and looked down at his hands.

"You-hoo, Jessie?" It was Beatrice coming up the back steps. "Jessie, I've brought over some of the goodies for this afternoon." She was trying to open the door.

Jessie got up from her seat. "Just a minute, Bea, and I'll help you." She opened the door. Beatrice was breathing hard and talking at the same time. "We've got so much to do. Grady and the others are cleaning off the grounds. Dick dropped me by; I'm not going to drive in this mess. And whose car is that in your driveway?" It was a storm of questions and statements. Bea walked into the den and saw James as he stood.

"Oh my!" she said. "I didn't expect . . . I didn't know . . . um, you're James, right?"

Jessie walked in behind her and took the dish from her hands. "Bea, this is my ex-husband, James Jenkins."

Bea looked flustered. "Oh my, I should have called first. I hadn't expected anyone and Dick was going to the store so he stopped by and offered to bring me here; he's getting some more stuff out of the car."

"Bea, it's fine. We were just talking." Jessie rolled her eyes at James.

"Well, of course you were just talking. I didn't mean to imply you were doing anything other than talking." She couldn't stop herself.

"Pleased to see you again, Bea. It's been a long time." James shook her hand.

"I'll say it's been a long time. What, twenty years?" She turned to share a laugh with Jessie, but Jessie wasn't laughing.

"Oh, there I go again. Sometimes I have a nervous habit of talking too much. Do you have any nervous habits, Jessie?" She pulled her hand away from James.

"Oh, I think so," Jessie said as she looked over at all the things she had baked.

Beatrice followed her eyes towards the kitchen. "Oh, Mexican wedding cookies!" She walked over to the counter.

Dick Witherspoon was coming in the door. "Knock, knock," he said.

"Oh, just come in. Look, Dick, Jessie made Mexican wedding cookies."

She reached for the dishes he was carrying, and before he could reply, she turned back to Jessie. "He makes the best Mexican wedding cookies. In fact, I'm going to put his recipe in our book. Won't that be nice?" She smiled over at Dick and then at Jessie.

Dick reached out his hand to Jessie. "Congratulations on this event."

Jessie said, "Thank you," then introduced him to James, who also shook the funeral director's hand, which was cold and clammy.

"You from D.C.?" Dick moved closer to the other man while the women began to arrange the dishes in the kitchen. They started to talk about the Washington area, where Dick had lived a few years.

Beatrice smiled and winked at Jessie like she knew a secret. Jessie just shook her head and laughed. Then she lifted her eyebrows in a question mark towards Dick. Beatrice knew the meaning and just slapped Jessie on the hand and blushed. "He's really much more cultured than I imagined," she whispered, and Jessie nodded. "We're thinking about going to Europe in March." She giggled. "Won't that be the talk of

Hope Springs?" And she waved her hand around.

"Well, I've got a few more dishes to get from the car, then I've got to go pick up the cake, go by and fix Roxie's hair and makeup, do my own, finish fixing the punch, and get back to the church in less than two hours!" She looked frantic. "How can you be so calm?" And she headed out the door before Jessie could answer.

"Well, I guess I better get the car turned around and moving in the right direction before Beatrice is stuck without her blush and curlers!" Dick said his good-byes, handed Jessie the two dishes that Beatrice had given him at the back door, and left.

"Nice folks." James smiled with an air of uncertainty.

"Salt of the earth," Jessie responded.

"I have my clothes for the wedding in the car. If it's all right, I'll just change here and drive you to the church." He was all tender and vulnerable again, and Jessie was blinded by it like it was a storm of snow.

"Yeah, that will be fine. You can even help Wallace with his tie." Jessie looked at her watch.

"Oh, I better start getting ready myself. Wallace should be home soon. You can help yourself to anything to eat if you like. I'll be in the back getting dressed."

James followed his ex-wife with his eyes as she went down the hall and into the bedroom they once had shared. He sighed, poured himself another cup of coffee, and took a cookie from the platter. He stood in front of the kitchen window as memories stirred in his mind and he was warmed by the possibilities.

Jessie shut the door and leaned back against it. She thought about James, the way he looked, the years they had been apart. He seemed settled in a way that he hadn't been in a long time. Something felt ironed out, smoothed down and pressed flat. It was as if nothing was in his way anymore. Jessie didn't know what was different or what if anything the change meant, but she liked the way it felt. She liked that he was there, standing in her kitchen. And she liked it that, for whatever reason, he seemed right at home.

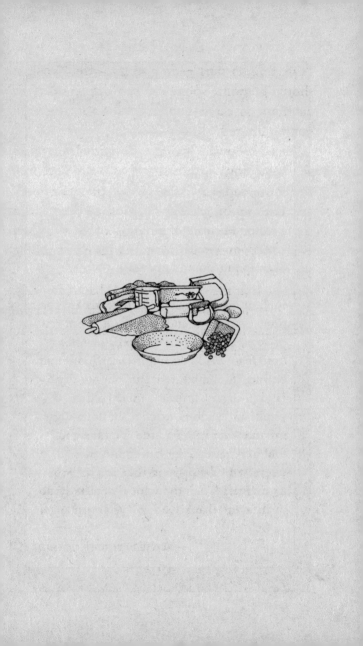

Roxie's Angel Food Cake

¾ cup cake flour
¼ cup sugar
10 to 12 egg whites
1 teaspoon cream of tartar
1 teaspoon vanilla
½ teaspoon almond extract

Preheat oven to 350°F. Sift together two or three times flour and half of sugar. Sift rest of sugar and set aside. Whip egg whites until foamy. Add cream of tartar. Continue beating until mixture is stiff but not dry. Fold in sugar a little at a time. Fold in vanilla and almond extract. Sift flour-sugar mixture over batter a little at a time and fold into batter. Pour batter into an ungreased tube pan and bake at 350°F for 45 minutes. Then top with chocolate syrup or fruit and thank God you've got an angel.

—ROXIE BARNETTE CANNON

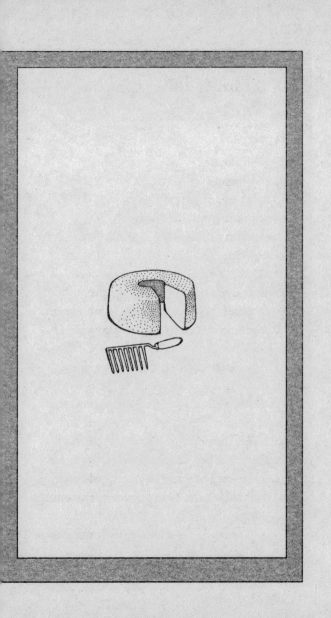

On that blustery day in December, Hope Springs Community Church was crowded with well-wishers and church members to celebrate the wedding of Wallace Jenkins and Lana Sawyer.

Dick Witherspoon and Beatrice Newgarden stood at the door to greet the folks and pass out bulletins. It was noticed that during most of the service, the music and the speaking of the vows, Dick and Bea were holding hands.

Roxie and Louise sat near the back, and Roxie could be heard singing during a couple of the hymns. Margaret stood in the narthex, beaming with pride that her church had managed a miracle and that the wedding party remembered where they were supposed to stand and how they were to march in and out.

Charlotte was relaxed and at ease, even giving an impromptu thank-you to everyone who had weathered the storm and was present for the ritual.

Jessie sat with James and loved the nearness of his arm both beside and around her. Lana and Wallace were nervous as cats but somehow managed to say the vows and follow directions without a hitch.

The wedding was one of the most beautiful Hope Springs had ever hosted; everybody said so. And the reception at Jessie's was packed with people and overflowing with joy. No one believed that the community would be able to laugh so soon after their tears, but it felt easy and necessary, and the people obliged their hearts.

It was a glorious day for the Hope Springs community, and afterwards the Cookbook Committee sat in Jessie's den while a few family members stood around in the kitchen. Louise had taken Roxie into a bedroom for a nap since she kept falling asleep on the sofa. She was coming out when she heard Jessie ask the group how Roxie was doing.

"She's worse." Louise got herself a cup of punch and sat down next to Beatrice. "But today was a good day. It was a really good day." She smiled at Jessie, who nodded back at her.

"I heard her singing 'Here Comes the Bride.' I didn't even know there were words to 'Here Comes the Bride.' " Margaret was nibbling on a piece of cake.

"I'm not sure there are words, and even if there are, I'm not sure they were the words Roxie was singing." Louise took a bite of her friend's cake.

"She seems really content, Lou." Beatrice was fanning herself.

"Yeah, she's satisfied, I think; I mean, with being here." Louise saw Jessie looking in the kitchen, soaking in James with her eyes. "You still got it for your old man?"

Jessie was surprised at the question, surprised that everyone had figured out her secret admiration. She blushed. "You've got to admit, he still looks good."

James glanced into the den and noticed that the women were watching him. He raised his cup and grinned.

"He looks all right, I suppose." It was Beatrice. "If you like that sort of run off and forget you kind of guy."

"Oh, Bea. Leave them alone. Jessie's a grown woman. She knows what she wants." Margaret offered Louise another bite of cake.

"You mean, she knows *who* she wants." And Beatrice put her cup to her mouth, her little finger balancing the weight.

"No, I think it's more like *what* I want." Jessie licked her lips while the other women laughed. James turned back towards the women.

"Girl, I do know about that." Beatrice put down her cup and looked over at Dick, who was sitting at the kitchen table flipping through a magazine.

Louise and Margaret exchanged glances.

"Really, Bea, you? I never had you figured for the, um," Jessie struggled for a word.

"Horny type." It was Louise who finished the sentence.

They all laughed. Beatrice seemed unbothered. "Well, a woman does have needs." She gave a dainty wave towards Dick, who smiled back at her.

"Don't you think it's a little weird being with a funeral director? I mean, has he asked you to do it in a coffin?" Louise whispered the question, and the women howled. Everybody in the kitchen looked their way.

Charlotte walked over before anyone could respond. "And just what is the raucous topic for today's committee meeting?"

The women laughed again. "Sex," said Margaret.

"Oh?" said an embarrassed Charlotte. "Maybe I need to skip out on this meeting then."

"No, it's plenty appropriate for a preacher's ears." And Louise motioned Charlotte to join her on the sofa. "Jessie here was only saying that she was glad to have James back."

Charlotte looked at Jessie, then over to James. She seemed to like the thought of the two of them back together.

"And we know about Dick and Bea." She smiled at Beatrice, proud that she was finally using first names with the women. "So what about you two, Margaret and Louise?"

Margaret cleared her throat and shook her head with a laugh. "Not anything to know, Preacher. I'm used to living alone, and I can't imagine being any other way. I'm perfectly content with the way things are."

Then they all looked at Louise, who started to get up from the couch. "I guess that's my cue to leave." And before anyone could ask another question, she walked into the bedroom and roused Roxie. After a few minutes the two of them were in coats and scarves, and Dick and Bea hurried to get ready so they could take them home.

"I think I'll be leaving too." Charlotte hugged Jessie. "It was a great day, a beautiful wedding." And she waited for Margaret, since the two of them came together.

One by one they said good-bye until only James and Jessie were left. Lana and Wallace were staying the night at the Embassy Suites in town, a gift from Louise and Roxie.

Jessie waved good-bye to everyone, closed and locked the door, and began cleaning up the dishes. James went into the kitchen and stood near Jessie as she put on an apron.

"That wasn't a bad party, for white people, I mean." James smiled and started rolling up his sleeves.

"Yeah, I thought it turned out real nice." She plugged the drain in the sink and turned on the water.

James reached below, got the dishwashing detergent, and poured a little in the sink.

Jessie watched with surprise as he put the container back where he found it.

"You know, the children are going to talk about this." She reached in the water to find the dishcloth. She felt his fingers stop and spread apart while she moved hers across his.

"So then maybe I should go?" He turned to face her.

"I suppose you will eventually anyway." Jessie pulled her hands from the water and dried them on her apron.

"I don't know," he said. "You're right about Washington. I'm too old for the job, and I'm too old for the city." He reached for her hands. "I think I'd like to stay."

Jessie was surprised, but she let him keep her hands. Water trickled across his fingers onto hers. "What made you go the first time?"

He looked down and then back into her eyes. "I got no excuse for what I did." He caught a stream of water as it dripped down her arm. "Except I always felt like you were too good for me, Jess." He dried her arm with the towel. "No matter how hard I tried, it always seemed like I was letting you down."

She turned away, pulling the towel from his hands. "You broke my heart, James Jenkins. That's what you did. You broke it as sure as we're standing here." A tear fell from her eye.

"Yeah," he said, as he turned her face towards his. "I know that." He looked into her eyes, captured her there. "I'm sorry." He pulled her towards him, and there were no more words. He would be staying the rest of the night.

WHEN LOUISE GOT Roxie home and in bed, she could tell that there had been a change in her breathing. Nothing very labored or drastic, but it seemed she breathed less, took in less air. She got the notebook and began to write down the things from the wedding and reception, then went back into the room where Roxie was sleeping.

Roxie opened up her eyes and looked at Louise. "You're my angel, Louie, and I want to stay here with you."

Louise reached over and touched Roxie on

the cheek. "Of course you will stay here." She kissed her forehead, and Roxie closed her eyes.

Louise thought about sleeping in the room with her, sitting in the chair next to Roxie, but she was so tired from the day, she fell asleep in her bed before she could make a decision.

She awoke late the next morning and was surprised to find that Roxie had not wakened her with yells to go to the bathroom. She glanced at the clock. It was well past 9:00. She looked out the window; the snow was still covering the ground.

"You had a big day yesterday, young lady," Louise was saying as she walked up the hallway towards the den. She was still wearing her pajamas.

She went into the kitchen first, poured a glass of juice, and got Roxie's morning medications. "You were singing and carrying on at the wedding like it was *your* big day." She walked into the den and stopped. Roxie was pale, unmoving. Louise put down the juice and the pills and reached for Roxie's arm to take a pulse. There was nothing. Roxie didn't breathe or flutter her eyelids or smile. She was dead.

There were no screams, not even tears. Louise laid her head on Roxie's chest, listening for a breath or a heartbeat, but the woman's body was empty of any life. Louise stood up, reached beside the bed for a brush, and fixed Roxie's hair. Then she went into the bathroom, got a washcloth and towel, and gave Roxie a sponge bath. She cleaned her with great care. Louise then put on her own clothes, dressed Roxie in a sweatshirt and sweatpants, and fluffed the pillows behind her head. She made no sound. It was a silent, independent series of actions, pieces of an intimate friendship, tokens of love. She cleaned up around the bed and sat down at the telephone to make calls.

First she spoke to George and then the children. She was informative and sympathetic. She waited until the shock wore off for each one, asking if they were okay, reminding them how much Roxie loved them, and how attentive they had been as her family, and then, with a professional and caring tone, she hung up the phone. Afterwards she called the doctor, who sent out an EMT and a deputy sheriff. She called Margaret, who came over immediately, and Dick, who came dressed in jeans and a sweater, since he knew Louise would feel more comfortable with him dressed like this than if he were in a suit.

Charlotte arrived just minutes after the funeral home personnel. She was late because she had walked from the parsonage. When she got to the house, Jessie and James were taking down the hospital bed and Beatrice was fixing a pot of coffee. Margaret and Louise were sitting in the den.

"I'm sorry it took me so long, I couldn't get my car to start." Charlotte took off her hat and gloves. "Guess it's the cold weather."

"Where's your car now?" Beatrice asked as she peered out the kitchen window.

"I walked," she said.

"Walked?" Margaret got up to take the rest of her wet clothes. "That's got to be five miles or more!"

"Four and a half. But it's okay. I find it stimulating." Charlotte pulled off her coat, handed it to Margaret, and knelt down in front of Louise.

"What happened?" Charlotte was flushed from the exercise and the cold.

"I don't know. I slept in my bed last night. I was planning to come back in here; I don't know why I didn't. I fell asleep in my room, I guess." There was a long pause.

"When I got up this morning, she . . ." Louise thought for a minute. It seemed as if she was re-membering something. "She said last night she wanted to stay with me. I didn't know what she meant. I didn't know she was planning to . . ." Her voice dropped.

Margaret sat back on the sofa, reached over, and put Louise's head on her shoulder.

"George wants to take her back to Maryland. They have plots up there." She sat up and wiped her eyes. "So I guess that's that."

Beatrice whispered to the other women. "Dick said he's to ship the body tonight or to-morrow. The funeral home up there is taking care of the arrangements."

Jessie was placing the bed rails on top of the bed when she noticed a piece of paper stuck be-hind the headboard. She pulled it out while Louise watched. "It looks like a recipe of some kind." She handed it to Louise.

"It's for angel food cake. She loved that." She read over the list of ingredients. "I knew she had written something those first few weeks she was here, but she wouldn't show it to me. I thought it was a letter to George. She must have heard our conversations about the book."

Margaret glanced over her shoulder at the handwritten paper.

"It looks like she didn't get finished." Louise showed Margaret. There was a list of instructions that ended with using an ungreased tube pan and baking at 350 degrees, but the rest of the words she couldn't read.

"Oh, the rest is easy." Beatrice came over and reached for the paper. "It looks like top it with something," she studied it, "but I can't make it out."

Louise took it back, knowing what it said without reading it, "chocolate sauce and fruit." She turned to Beatrice. "It was her favorite." Then she looked back at the recipe. "But what about here, what does it say here?" And she pointed to the last line, which was written with a very shaky hand.

The women passed the paper around, each one trying to decipher a word or a few letters.

"And think sad . . ." Jessie had it and passed it on to Charlotte.

"And think God you've, something, anger?" She handed it to Beatrice, who studied it awhile, then gave it back to Margaret, who was still sitting beside Louise.

"And thank God you've got an angel." Margaret read it, the words tight and sure, then she smiled at Louise, who sat back and cried.

Elizabeth's Christmas Moravian Cakes

½ pound dark brown sugar
1 pint molasses
½ cup lard
1 stick butter
1 tablespoon cinnamon
1½ teaspoons cloves
1½ teaspoons ginger
1½ teaspoons baking soda
8 cups sifted all-purpose flour

Add sugar to molasses and mix well. Add lard and butter, melted and cooled. Sift spices and soda with a little flour and add to the molasses mixture, stirring in well. Then add the rest of the flour until you have a stiff dough. Let stand overnight. Roll thinly on a floured board. Cut into shapes with cookie cutters, and bake on greased tins in moderate oven (350°F). This recipe makes about 3 pounds. Baking time is about 9 minutes.

—ELIZABETH GARNER

*E*lizabeth Garner was the one who broke the news to the rest of the Cookbook Committee about Louise camping out at the cemetery. It was the day before Christmas Eve. Margaret had taken Louise up to Maryland for the funeral over four days ago. She was at her wit's end since Louise wouldn't come home. She called Elizabeth because she wanted to ask her son, the EMT, how long somebody could stay outside in the cold without getting frostbite. Margaret told Elizabeth that they needed to leave Maryland, but Louise wouldn't listen and she wouldn't come in from the cold. Elizabeth heard the panic in the otherwise calm Margaret and called the preacher immediately.

There were no questions asked, no plans made. The women set out for Maryland to try to help Margaret and Louise. Jessie and Charlotte took turns driving while Beatrice served as navigator. They got lost outside Richmond, but they were still able to get to George's house in less than six hours. When they arrived, Margaret was cooking an early supper. George and his girlfriend had gone to stay at her house, since things were a little awkward with Louise visiting.

The women walked into the house and were surprised to find Margaret alone. She was glad to see them.

She appeared frayed, stringy, like an old rug. "She's at the grave. She hasn't left since the day after the funeral."

She walked back to the stove. "We've tried everything. The funeral director talked to her. The preacher sent some suicide chaplain out there. George and the children tried to get her to leave. I even stayed with her a couple of nights, but I couldn't stand it anymore. She's planning on spending Christmas Eve out there, for God's sake."

Margaret pulled out drawers trying to find a spoon. "She does eat, at least. I take her meals to her, something warm to drink, and she goes into the church to relieve herself. They've been nice enough to leave the back door open."

The women shuffled in and began taking off hats and gloves. They all stood near the table while Margaret went back around the counter to the stove. When she threw the lid of a pot into the sink, it slammed and rattled, and the women froze in their places. "She's lost her damn mind, and I don't know what I'm going to do."

Jessie waited a minute, then went over to the stove and adjusted the burners. She picked up a spoon and stirred the soup, which was starting to boil over. Beatrice walked over to Margaret, putting her arm around her and leading her back to the table.

Charlotte looked towards Jessie, unsure of what to do next. Jessie nodded, a sign to say something, so she asked, "Why don't you tell us about the funeral and how Louise was doing with everything?"

Margaret sat at the table as Charlotte pulled out chairs for Beatrice and herself.

"Things seemed fine, I thought." Margaret wiped her brow with the back of her hand. "We stayed here with George. He's not a bad guy, you know?" She said this to Beatrice. "Lou was civil, didn't say much, seemed like she was okay."

Jessie poured Margaret a glass of water, handed it to her, and leaned back against the counter.

"The service was sweet. The preacher did a nice job." She turned towards Charlotte, who nodded. "It was short. The songs were appropriate. Everything was fine. And then, when we were at the grave, her face just changed. It became frozen, glass. Like she had made up her mind about something."

Margaret shook her head. "We came back from the service, and she went into the garage. She didn't say anything to anybody. We heard her putting some things in the trunk, and then she just drove off without a word. I figured she needed some time alone, so I didn't get worried until it started getting dark. Then George and the boys and I drove around searching for her. We went everywhere in town. But we found her at the grave." Margaret faced Jessie. "She's been there ever since." And she took a swallow of water.

Charlotte put her hand on top of Margaret's. "You okay?"

Margaret shrugged her shoulders and nodded unconvincingly.

The women glanced around at each other. Then, without hesitation, Beatrice responded. "Well, there's nothing else to do but go out there and talk to her." She reached over, patted Margaret on the arm, slipped her coat back on, buttoned it up, and headed out the door.

Margaret sighed. "Here, let me write down the directions to the church." She found some paper and a pen, jotted down some instructions, and handed the paper to Charlotte.

"You stay here; we'll do something, even if it's wrong," said Jessie.

Margaret just watched as Jessie and Charlotte left to join Beatrice.

THE SUN WAS beginning to fade, and the temperature was dropping. Louise was sitting under the green funeral tent, next to the grave, in a lawn chair, the long kind you use at the beach. She was surrounded by arrangements of frozen flowers and under several layers of blankets, wearing two pairs of gloves, a thick scarf about her neck, and an old army helmet strapped on her head. She was singing "A Hundred Bottles of Beer on the Wall," when her friends walked up. She was on "Seventy-three bottles."

Jessie shook her head in amazement. "Girl, you have definitely gone over the edge."

Louise looked over her shoulder. She smiled. "Well, well, well, if it isn't the Cookbook Committee. Roxie, what do you think of that?" She faced the grave, the new dirt already frozen hard. Then she turned back to Beatrice. "Queen Bea, you having trouble with another recipe?"

The women looked at each other. They weren't sure if Louise was drunk or just crazy from the cold.

"No, we came to find you." Beatrice went and stood beside Louise.

Jessie moved closer too. "It's cold out here, Lou."

Louise nodded. "Yep. But after a while you start to lose feeling. It's not so cold then." She handed Jessie one of her blankets. "Margaret still at George's?"

"Yes," said Beatrice. "She was fixing you some soup when we left."

Just then Charlotte came out with three fold-ing chairs. "I took them from the choir room," she said, somewhat out of breath. "Nice church."

Jessie helped her set them out and took a seat with Beatrice and Charlotte beside Louise.

They sat in silence for a few minutes. Suddenly Louise turned around to face the women. "Isn't tomorrow Christmas Eve?"

They all nodded.

"Don't you have someplace to be on Christmas Eve?"

There was another pause. "We came to be with you, Lou." It was Beatrice.

"Dick with you?" She handed Beatrice the thermos.

"No, he's with his sister in Winston-Salem." Beatrice opened the thermos and took a big gulp. She almost choked when she tasted the alcohol. She spat and sputtered. "Good God, Lou, is this straight whiskey?"

Louise smiled.

Jessie took the thermos. "You forgot who you were talking to, Bea." She took a small sip and passed it on to Charlotte, who seemed unsure of what to do.

"Louie, queen of the hooch, that's me!" And Louise whirled her hands in the air with a whooping noise.

Charlotte took a swallow. The liquor burned her throat, but she didn't cough or spit it up. Then she handed the thermos back to Jessie.

Louise looked over at Charlotte, who was now shifting her weight from side to side in the chair, trying to get warm. Then she pulled a flower out of an arrangement close by her head and twirled it in her hand. "I didn't like the preacher." She turned back towards the grave. "He was small and shifty, and his hands were sweaty. Reminded me of Dick."

Beatrice rolled her eyes.

"And he didn't know Rox. Not even a little." She dropped the flower in her lap and reached for the thermos. Jessie handed it to her. She took a swallow and put the top back on it. "He said things that you could tell were memorized, rehearsed. Stuff he could say about anybody, even you, Bea." She lifted her chin at Beatrice and smiled. Then the corners of her lips fell. "He didn't know anything about Rox."

Charlotte dropped her head, the scarf up to

the bottom of her nose. The wind was cold and stiff.

A group of carolers were meeting at the church to go out into the community. The women looked over as they chatted and laughed casually among themselves.

Louise started singing again, "Seventy-two bottles of beer on the wall, seventy-two bottles of beer . . ."

Jessie interrupted her. "What didn't he know about Rox that you could have told him, Lou?" And she gave Charlotte part of her blanket, pulling it around their legs.

The young people glanced towards the cemetery. A hush came over the group. All of the women but Louise turned and looked.

"That she was everything to me. The reason I stayed alive. The reason I stayed sane. The reason I thought the world wasn't such a bad place to live or that I wasn't somehow completely nuts. That she was the color in this drab, boring universe." Louise stopped, and no one said a word.

"Even when she was really sick, out of her mind sick, she filled the empty place. You know what I mean, Jess?" She looked over at the women. "You know what I mean? Roxie filled the empty place." She unscrewed the top of the thermos and took another drink.

"And even though she was never mine to have, and our worlds were so different, I can't see how I can possibly live without her." Her voice became choked and distant. "I don't even know how to breathe."

A wind stirred the flowers and caused the sides of the tent to flap against the poles. The carolers walked over to the women and began to sing "Silent Night." It was an empty, awkward gesture, and Beatrice stood up and stopped them in the middle of the second line, "All is calm, all is—"

"Excuse me," she said, and their voices trailed off like a swarm of bees.

"Here's what I'm thinking," she said as she slid her hands down the front of her coat and pulled on the top of her hat. The other women were wide-eyed and still.

"I'm thinking you got four women, obviously in some distress, sitting in the freezing cold in a cemetery." Her voice was strong and brassy. She was a trumpet of bad news. "I'm thinking the last thing they need to hear is some sentimental hogwash Christmas song that reminds them of everybody dead they've ever known. So I'm thinking maybe it would be a better idea if you go and sing to somebody who's not nearly so desperate and pushed to the outer limits of what might be deemed appropriate behavior."

She clasped her gloved hands in front of her like an opera singer who's just finished her solo. "Does what I'm thinking seem clear enough for you?"

And the young people, stunned, pulled off their red-and-green happy hats, each with tiny tinkling bells on the end, and jingled back to the church, dejected and unsure of what to do next.

Suddenly, Louise began to laugh. Charlotte and Jessie eyed each other and laughed too. Beatrice, spent from her lecture, sat back down and took the thermos for a long, tasty drink.

Just then Margaret drove into the parking lot, got out of the car, waved at the carolers, and walked towards the women with a pot of steaming soup. She had not expected there to be laughter; by this time it was building and full. "Obviously, I missed something."

Charlotte got up to help her with the pot and bowls. "Yep, I would say you definitely missed something." She turned to Beatrice, who was wiping her mouth with the back of her arm. She turned back to Margaret. "Let me help you with that." And Charlotte dipped a bowl of soup for everyone. She handed the first one to Louise.

"Why is it that when you're feeling the least like eating, people bring you food?" She held the bowl in her lap. "I mean, why don't folks bring you casseroles when things are going great? Why don't people want to sit around with you and eat potato salad when you get a promotion or win the lottery? Why, when someone has died, does everyone suddenly have to bake a cake?"

"I always enjoy the food at funerals." Charlotte motioned for the thermos from Beatrice, and the women watched with surprise as she downed the last of the drink.

"I think we do it because it's all we got." Jessie took a spoonful of soup, blew on it, and continued. "Words are empty. There sure aren't any presents to buy, but everybody's got to eat, so we feed each other. It's the basic, most humane way to say you care.

"It's a silly ritual, I agree. But somehow it helps to remind ourselves that life goes on. We sit together. We remember. We eat."

Beatrice drank from her bowl, then put it down, wrapping herself in the blanket Jessie had given her.

"It's a way to dole out friendship, Lou. In your words, it's just doing what love does." And Margaret sat down on the end of the lawn chair, almost tipping them over.

"Yeah," Louise said. "I did say that once, didn't I?"

They sat for a while finishing their soup and listening as the carolers sang at the houses close by. They would laugh every time they heard "Silent Night."

Finally the youth group finished their singing, came back to the church, got in their cars, and left. It was dark and quiet and starting to snow. The women looked around at each other.

Louise felt the glances and spoke. "I know I have to go." She pulled off her helmet. "It's silly to think Roxie is here. She would never stay here, even as a dead person. It's much too gray and ugly, and forgive me, Preacher," she looked over to Charlotte, who was starting to nod off but opened her eyes wide when she heard the word *Preacher*—"but it's much too close to the church. Roxie would rather be in a park or by a lake or near friends talking, oh, I don't know, about a cookbook."

She cleared her throat. "I'm ready to go." She stood up by her chair. Margaret got up at the same time and stood behind the lawn chair. "But I don't know what I'll do about Christmas."

"You don't have to do anything about Christmas." Margaret stepped outside the tent, looking up at the North Star, which was shining in the sky, high and alone. "You'll come stay with me."

"Or me." It was Beatrice.

"Mom's coming over, but other than her and me, the parsonage is empty." Charlotte yawned and picked up the bowls and empty thermos.

The women looked at Jessie, waiting for her invitation. "Well, don't think you can come to my house. My bedrooms are full!" She gave a wicked grin and winked at Louise.

The women pulled the blankets around themselves and stood in a huddle behind Louise as she said a final good-bye to her friend. She folded up her blanket and threw it on the chair. Then she knelt down, whispered something to the frozen earth, gently kissed her hand, and patted the fresh grave. They watched as Charlotte took flowers from one of the wreaths, tied them stem to stem, and placed them around Louise's shoulders like a stole. It covered her like a blessing, and there, in the presence of women she loved, both dead and alive, Louise rose up and slowly started to breathe.

Lucy's Friendship Cake

CAKE

1 box Duncan Hines butter cake mix
1 small package instant vanilla pudding
  (4 ounces)
½ cup oil
½ cup water
½ cup creme sherry
1 cup pecans, finely chopped
4 eggs

BOILED DRESSING

¾ cup sugar
¾ stick butter
3 tablespoons sherry
3 tablespoons water

Place all cake ingredients in mixing bowl.
Mix on slow speed for 1 minute, then on
medium speed for 3 minutes or until well
mixed. Pour into a well-greased and floured

tube pan. Bake at 325°F for 1 hour. (Test to see if done with toothpick.)

Boil dressing ingredients 2 to 3 minutes. Pour over hot cake while still in pan. Let cake cool completely in pan.

—LUCY SEAL

"Bea, this better be a quick meeting. That baby is just about ready to come, and I expect to be there with my family to celebrate its arrival." Jessie was breathing hard, having walked briskly, as she entered the pastor's study.

Spring was starting to show itself about the place. Flowers were beginning to bloom. The fruit trees were budding, and the cookbook was just about completed.

"It will be, I promise." Beatrice had a stack of recipes and had made copies for all the committee members. "I don't have a lot of time myself since I've got to start packing for my trip."

Margaret was sitting next to Louise, who replied, "Here's what I'm thinking, Bea."

And they all laughed.

"I'm thinking," she continued, "that you will be living in sin if you travel the European continent with a man to whom you aren't married."

Beatrice rolled her eyes and flipped through the pages. "It's Lucy Seal." She wasn't paying Louise any attention.

"I'm thinking," Louise kept on, "that Dick Witherspoon better be a decent gentleman and have two rooms for you in every hotel."

"Do you mind, Louise? I'm trying to conduct a meeting." Everyone could tell that she was enjoying the teasing.

"What's the problem with Lucy Seal now?" Margaret hushed Louise.

"Let me guess, another pear dish swimming in wine coolers?" Jessie flipped through her copies.

Beatrice put Charlotte's papers on her desk. She was already at the hospital with Lana and Wallace, but she had opened the church so that they could meet in her office.

"Worse." She tapped the edges of the papers in her lap, trying to get them even. "Her friendship cake."

"Mm," Margaret responded. "That's a tough one."

"The last time she brought one of those to a women's meeting, Byron Garner was dispatched four times, all alcohol related." Jessie fanned herself with the pages.

"Peggy DuVaughn got pulled over by the sheriff for going over the yellow line," added Louise.

"And we all know what happened to Vastine when he took a few bites." Beatrice glanced around the room.

"Detox." They all said it together.

"Friendship cake"—Jessie studied the recipe—"it's such a hearty name for a cake. But exactly why is it called that?"

"Because sherry makes you friendly?" Louise asked.

Beatrice rolled her eyes. "No, Hoochie Louie, I think it has to do with how much cake the recipe makes, that it's so filling you have to share it with friends. And," she added with resolve, "it lasts a very long time, well, if it's kept in the refrigerator."

"Yeah, but sherry does still make you more friendly," replied Louise.

Margaret laughed. "I like it. I think it would be a great last recipe for the book."

Lynne Hinton

"Then we'll keep it," reported Beatrice as she read over the list of ingredients.

They all shuffled through the pages.

"We could add another recipe by the same name." Louise said this tenuously as she raised her shoulders as if posing a question.

"Meaning?" Beatrice asked.

"Meaning, we have a real recipe for friendship cake, and then we make up one."

"You mean, like those corny 'happy home recipes'?" Margaret was surprised to hear this idea coming from Louise.

"Well, it doesn't have to be corny." Louise folded her arms across her chest, her papers almost falling out of her lap.

"So what would you put in a recipe for a cake of friendship, Ms. Pastry Chef?" Jessie put her copies by the side of her chair.

"Tenacity," Louise said, half question, half statement, looking over at Bea. "You know, stick-to-itiveness, hanging in there with someone when she's over the deep end." She turned towards Margaret. "And loyalty, laughter. Lots of things."

"Well, look who has gone and gotten all mushy on us. Here at the final meeting of the

Cookbook Committee." Beatrice loved the irony of the suggestion.

"Oh, don't give her a hard time, Bea."

The phone rang. Jessie walked over to answer it. "I think it's a nice idea. Hope Springs Community Church," she said.

The women were quiet as Jessie listened to the news. Tears filled her eyes, and the others weren't sure if the news she was hearing was good or bad.

"Thank you. Thanks for calling. I'll be right there." She hung up the phone. "It was James." She reached for a tissue. "It's a little girl, and everybody's fine."

Margaret stood up and hugged Jessie. Louise and Beatrice gathered around her.

"I want to go on over there." She dabbed at her eyes. "You think you can finish this meeting without me?"

The women nodded their heads and smiled.

"And I like the idea of Lou's friendship cake," Jessie said to Louise. "But I would make sure that one ingredient is included."

The women waited while she handed Beatrice the papers, opened her purse, and pulled out her keys.

"Hope," she said. And Margaret took Louise's hand.

"Just like the name of this church and community and our newest, littlest member." She turned to all of her friends. "Hope." And she punched the air with her chin like the period at the end of a sentence and headed out the door.

Real Friendship Cake

───────◦◦◦───────

*Cooks' Note: This recipe takes extra preparation
and work.*

You will need a bunch of love, the kind
that is long-suffering and bears all things,
the kind that does not keep score of
mistakes or slips of the tongue. Blend this
with a serving of patience and add the
following ingredients.

A strong helping of backbone support is
necessary, for friendship is molded upon an
understanding that leaning is appropriate.

Fold in the promise to guard secrets and
the willingness to tell one's own.

Combine humor, the sweet taste of easy
laughter, and a fiery brand of loyalty to
keep the relationship firm.

A golden touch of the ability to sit in
silence will add to the overall consistency,
and a pinch of exuberant jubilation at the

sound of someone else's good news will add flavor.

Stir in a commitment of time and attention, and add a bit of surprise to taste.

Once the ingredients have been mixed together, treat this dish with care. And remember, this is the one cake that you can have and eat it too.

—THE COOKBOOK COMMITTEE OF THE HOPE
SPRINGS COMMUNITY CHURCH

Welcome to Pleasant Cross, North Carolina, home to Lynch's Mortuary, Shepherd's Grill, and three generations of the Ivy women. Admittedly headstrong, each of the Ivy women is blessed—and cursed—with a gift of Knowing. A captivating tale of small-town Southern life, Lynne Hinton's newest novel is infused with wisdom, a touch of mystery, and lessons to last a lifetime.

"Wise men will read it to learn and wise women will read it to remind themselves of things they know best. A lovely book."
Malachy McCourt,
author of *Singing My Him Song*

The Things I Know Best is now available in hardcover

*T*iny pieces of myself floated to the top of the glass, and I began to read my future in tea leaves. Mama and the preacher in the cabin by Sandy Creek, Liddy standing at the Trailways station near a bus going to Atlanta, Mr. Jenkins and the cut of his small, dark eyes, and some union of colors I don't yet recognize. Scrap by scrap, they all danced along the lip like memories in the wake of death. As they brooded and twitched, I stared down into my tomorrow wondering if I should drink from the cup or run to the sink and pour it out.

Reading hands is my sister's means of Knowing. Tiny crooked lines leading up and down, front to back, thumb to wrist, these are the roads she travels. Her fingers hot on your skin, she'll close her eyes, go all blind-looking, her lips counting marks, measuring curves and stops. She can give you the first letter of your lover's last name and open up the secrets of your heart. She's been touching palms since she was a little girl, understanding the life and death that people clutch in their fists in the name of love. By the time she turned nine, everybody in town knew she had the gift.

In spite of our recognizing it at such an early age, though, nobody treated her any more special than they did me. In our family, Knowing is a common sense; and even before I was sure like today that I had it, I knew stuff. All of the women have some form of it. Grandma Pino interprets the sky, predicts weather patterns, upcoming anomalies, drought, that sort of thing.

Aunt Doris reads dreams and can tell a pregnant woman the sex of her unborn child. Great-grandmother Lodie could heal troublesome ailments and call out evil spirits from the sick and cursed. And her mother before her, Big Lucille, was known to associate with ghosts.

All of the Ivy women have a little something extra that causes the people in town to have a healthy suspicion of our family. So the fact that I now see snatches of another day's events in my afternoon drink isn't frightening or alien; it merely establishes my gift in the parade of women who birthed me and brought me up.

Aunt Doris asked me when I was thirteen and had just started my period if I'd had any special dreams on the night before I'd seen blood. I thought back to what I'd dreamed: I remembered the softness of the ocean, the too-white tips of the waves; I saw myself swimming beneath the rocks and craggy coral with only one long, deep breath, felt a soft-finned dolphin rubbing against my thigh. But I didn't find it unusual enough to mention, since I'd had the dream twice before— both times marking some girlish passage. I shook my head no.

"Never you mind," she said, a cigarette balanced on her bottom lip. "You will Know best."

I suppose it would seem to any ordinary person that Knowing would make the women in our family rich or smart or at the very least well respected; but the truth is the Knowing hasn't given us anything extra. It seems, in fact, to have created a curse. All the Ivy women lean towards making bad decisions, especially when it comes to money and men. And just as we have accepted the ways we all Know, we also have accepted each other's poor choices in husbands and fathers for our children.

Daddy left when me and Liddy turned seven. Grandma came in the kitchen talking about the windstorm that was coming up while Liddy and Mama and me sat around the table watching the candles burn into the cake.

"JayDee left," Mama said, the words all square and neat. Then she blew out our candles. All fourteen of them in one quick, heavy breath. Liddy looked into her hands like she should have known, mad that she hadn't blown first. I just stuck my fingers into the side of the cake and pulled out the thickest pink rose.

I still remember the sweetness of the icing as it slid down my throat, and my mama's one lone tear snaking down her face.

"He ain't worth your water, Bertie," Grandma said as she reached into her pocket and pulled out a handkerchief. Handing it over, she added, "He had bad blood."

Mama's Knowing has a little more prestige than that of the others. She's the only one in the family who actually makes money from her gift. She foresees death. She gets an uneasy feeling that has something to do with the chirping of bats, that high-pitched way they fly around in the darkness; and somehow an image forms before her and she feels the slipping away of somebody's life, a beat stolen from her chest.

Mr. Lynch, from the funeral home, gives Mama a monthly allowance for her Knowing about death's arrival because he believes it gives them an edge on the planning of work schedules. By knowing in advance that funeral services will be needed, he can decide who can take a vacation and how many extra men are needed to work. He also knows who to call about delinquent monthly installments on pre-arranged plans. So Mr. Lynch feels it's well worth the hundred and fifty extra dollars a month he pays to Mama, on top of her regular wages. She also answers the phone and fills out insurance forms for him—tasks that are part of her job as the receptionist at the funeral home.

She's been working there for as long as I can remember; and the only death she's missed was the infant daughter of Janine Butler, who certainly wasn't meant to die.

Janine and Russell had gone on a vacation to Asheville in the fall five years ago. Nobody, not

even Mama, knew that a bear would steal a baby.
They searched the woods and campsites, valleys
and mountains, but never found the child. Russell came back to Pleasant Cross to clean out the
house and settle his debts, but Janine never came
home. To this day people say she walks unafraid
into the caves of bears, opening the mouths of
lions and pole cats, mountain after mountain,
looking for her baby girl.

I asked Mama if she believed that Little Etty
was still alive since there was never any sign
about the death; but she said the baby's last breath
had been so still and tiny that it hadn't attracted
the senses of the bats or the stirring within her
heart.

Secretly, I've always believed that Little Etty
Butler is not dead and is being raised by a clan of
bears in the Blue Ridge Mountains. She's growing like a cub, climbing trees, catching fish with
her hands, running through the meadow fast and
free, her thoughts and memories of a human life
dissolved into the dreams of a strong black bear.

Since there was no funeral for the little girl, no
arrangements to be made, Mama's pay wasn't
affected by this incident.

Liddy and me are now eighteen, just finished

General Lee High School and looking for which way to go. Liddy says she wants to head up north, try to make it in beauty school somewhere, grow a window-box garden, and find the boy who's meant for her, one whose last name begins with an O.

I haven't got such high ambition, never have. I feel comfortable being around people and things that are familiar. Mama and Aunt Doris agree that Liddy has the streak of desire and I have the stretch of satisfaction. It's true. I'm content not to know anything about tomorrow and to taste the sugar off birthday cakes even in the midst of personal tragedy.

Luther Shepherd, who owns Shepherd's Grill, offered me a job as a waitress serving breakfast and lunch. That seemed good enough for me. And it was here at the Grill, after today's shift, that I discovered the future, slippery in a glass of old tea, and began to worry about what would pass.

Liddy going to Atlanta—the first image my tea revealed—makes me sad and uneasy since we've never been separated. And yet it isn't like we didn't know she'd be going. She almost quit school at sixteen to take a job in Detroit she'd

heard about from the guidance counselor. She
had train schedules to New York and Washington; and she was thinking about riding up to
Boston with Leo Jacobs, who drove a truck up
there every other Thursday.

She's been planning to leave for as long as
we've been sisters, so it comes as no surprise that
the time is at hand. At least Atlanta isn't as far
away as New York or Boston.

Mama and the preacher, Reverend Lawson—
now seeing them together in my glass is a little
unnerving, even though I've seen the way he
looks at her during altar calls. His forehead gets
all sweaty when she walks down the aisle, and he
holds her tighter than the others when she
stands before him confessing some sin she can
never seem to get shed of.

Whenever I ask her what it is she's done that
she has to go down front every Sunday, she just
shakes her head and looks far away into some
past trouble that she won't name.

The preacher's wife doesn't like Mama much
and never speaks when she comes to the funeral
home with her husband. She gives us all the ice-
berg shoulder and a look down her nose that
makes me think maybe she's Lutheran or Pres

byterian and doesn't really want to be with the Baptists. Mama isn't too bothered by it, though; she says there's only one thing worse than a carousing, sex-starved preacher, and that's a married one.

The signs of this future event have been around for a long time too. So even though I know it will get her into a mess at the church, maybe even cost her her job, even that image doesn't cause me too much worry.

It's the look on Mr. Jenkins's face. The tightness of his breath. The mean curl of his lip as he cuts his eyes away from my Knowing image. This is the piece that stays on me. This and the arrival of some remnants of color I feel pleasure from but can't describe. Herein lies the predicament that I detect isn't all goodness.

Mr. Jenkins runs the savings and loan on the edge of downtown. He also owns just about everything and everybody in Pleasant Cross. His daddy, Olaf Jenkins, didn't trust banks and wouldn't set foot in one; so when the Great Depression hit and everybody lost their money, he had a nice stash in his barn that he loaned to people at a considerable interest.

When they couldn't pay him back, he took

possession of their farms, their houses, and any land they owned. Somebody said he even took a pet pig away from Curtis Murray when Mr. Murray couldn't pay back his debt and the house he lived in was rented. Took the pig and cooked it, stabbed it right in front of Mr. Murray's house while little Curtis stood on the porch and watched. Grandma says that's why Curtis is a railroad drunk today.

Mr. Olaf Jenkins had a surly reputation; and his sons, Donald and Tyrus, didn't fall far from the family tree. Donald died young many years ago when a tractor he'd repossessed for his father fell on top of him, getting, as all the folks say, what he deserved. Tyrus Jenkins, the banker, the one in my tea glass, is known to turn down loans to anybody he doesn't approve of, and that's about everybody in town. He's the mayor and the chair of the town council, and everybody owes him something.

So you see, he's not a man to dream of or think much about; and he's certainly not a person you want to see floating in the pictures of your future.

"You ready to go home?" Liddy, who has a job over at Tina's House of Beauty, has covered her eyelids with eye shadow. She bats her long black lashes at me. "It's Silk Lapis. Do you think I look like a rock singer?"

She's just the same as me, long-armed and skinny, clumsy feet, sharp bones, and a thin oval face. Only she wears a lot more makeup, colors her hair, and shops at the mall.

"You look like you rubbed Easter eggs all over your eyes." I say this as I yank off my Shepherd's Grill apron and throw it in the basket of dirty linens by the trash can.

Luther, taking a breather during the after-lunch lull, pulls a toothpick from his mouth and peeks up over the afternoon newspaper. "Tessa Lucille, don't forget you got to refill the ketchup bottles first thing in the morning."

"Yeah," I answer.

"Why does he call you all that?" Liddy whispers. She erases the date and the special of the day off the chalkboard before we leave and writes, "Today is the fist day of the rest of your life." (Spelling wasn't her best subject in school, and she rarely looks over what she's done.)

I shrug in answer to her question and decide not to correct the error. I grab my jacket off the coat tree, knowing that it's way too hot to wear it now but remembering that it'll be cold at five-thirty tomorrow morning, even though it's summer.

Liddy is happy. I can tell by the way she's walking. Light and airy like the ballerina in our homeroom. We always tried to walk like Elizabeth Hines. She had blond hair that she tied up in a tight bun, and she never seemed to look down. She wasn't so very tall, but it always felt as if she was a head above everybody else. She carried herself like she was the daughter of royalty. We'd practice at home with a book on our heads or a roll of paper towels under our chins, hoping to look like her. But we were never able to walk with that kind of pride and instead just looked like we were trying to show off our breasts.

Elizabeth got a scholarship to the School of the Arts and left early in the spring to travel up north before her college began. There was something about her being real smart that they let her leave two months before high school was over. Or maybe it was that the art school didn't care if she had a diploma or not; they were just worried that her knees might get damaged in PE.

Anyway, looking at Liddy now, I think that

maybe she practiced when I wasn't around, because she seems so tall and righteous.

"I'm going to Albuquerque," she says suddenly, stopping and turning right towards me, her chest high and puffed out. "That's in New Mexico."

"I know where it is," I say. And I'm unsure now if maybe I misread the leaf with Liddy's life on it. Maybe I mixed up the towns that start with A. "What's in New Mexico?"

"Tina's cousin's family." Liddy is looking at herself in Clifford's Used Bookstore window. She's rubbing the blue up to her brow and shaping it with a finger that she licked for just that purpose.

"Liddy, you don't even like Tina. What makes you think you're going to want to stay with her cousins?"

"First off," she says, turning around, her eyes like two drops of water—clean ocean water that won't spill—"I never said that I didn't like Tina. I just said that she should have never dyed her hair that burgundy color and that she really didn't have a flair for fashion. And second, I won't be staying with her cousins that long—just until I can find a place of my own."

"Here." Liddy licks her finger again, takes
swoop of Silk Lapis from her right lid, an
smears it on mine.

I roll back my head and close my eyes as sh
paints me. When I look up and see ourselves i
the window, we're the same. Only each outsid
eye is shaded in blue. We're one big woman wit
arms and legs on the inside that we don't need.

"When are you going?"

"Sometime in July, maybe August. I'm goin
to do nails at Tina's during the day and cashier ;
Cordessa's every night but Monday. I can wor
two shifts on Friday and Saturday." Liddy turr
to walk back up the street towards the funer;
home.

"I figure in eight weeks I can save about fif
teen hundred bucks. That should get me goin
in Albuquerque." She's about ten steps ahead c
me.

"Cordessa's?" I ask, hurrying to get beside he
"Cordessa's?" Have you told Mama?" I wipe th
sweat off my forehead. I can't believe what I'r
hearing.

"I'll tell her tonight." Her tone is firm, but he
shoulders aren't quite as tall as they were in fror
of the bookstore.

I look at her in disbelief.

She looks back, sort of haughty-like. "Tessa, we're eighteen now. Mama can't tell us what to do anymore."

We stop at the intersection, then turn in the direction of the funeral home.

"Being eighteen don't mean anything to Mama when it comes to Cordessa," I say. We cross another street and head into Mr. Lynch's parking lot.

Liddy doesn't say anything back to this because she knows it's true. Mama has some sort of weird disposition towards Cordessa Pender.

The most I can put together is that Mama and Cordessa were best friends growing up. In spite of the fact that Mama is white and Cordessa is black, they were always thicker than thieves and closer than sisters. That's what Aunt Doris says. They were even almost related, since Aunt Doris's son, our cousin Jasper, was living with Cordessa's daughter, Millie, before she died in that train wreck in Florida.

Millie's death was a sad and shocking event for the family. And Mama wouldn't go to the funeral, even though she knew about it before everybody else since she heard the bats and then

saw Cordessa walk by the funeral home with
cloud passing over.

I remember that church day as a time o
intense negotiations between Mama and Doris
Aunt Doris claimed that Mama owed it to th
family to be there in support of Jasper and tha
she needed to let the past be healed. Mama jus
turned to her sister and told her in that rea
quiet, serious voice that she'd better leave.

That's when I first heard about the "incident
between Mama and her growing-up friend
Liddy and I asked Grandma while she was out
side checking the skies with her wet finge
pointed to heaven what had happened so man
years ago that Mama couldn't forgive. Grandm
wouldn't say much except that Cordessa an
Mama had lost themselves in some storm tha
nobody had foreseen or understood. And tha
some things were just meant to be left unknowr

She said it like she'd rehearsed this answe:
repeated it so many times, to herself I guess, tha
she'd finally come to accept it.

Mama dropped out of school and went t
work at Lynch's, although she'd been plannin
to go to the nursing college in Greensboro.
guess she packaged up her pain and inability t

move beyond Pleasant Cross, North Carolina, and labeled it Cordessa Pender.

It appears that even though Mama wears sadness like a second skin and seems to be always trying to rid herself of it, she's going to stay covered if getting free means she has to fix things with Cordessa.

Cordessa graduated, they say, and married Max years and years ago but apparently left him after she bought the bar on the interstate. Mr. Pender still lives in their house back behind the tire plant. He was at Millie's funeral sitting with Cordessa, quiet and limp, moving like an old dog trying to find a place to rest. Aunt Doris had the family over to her house after, since everyone knew it was awkward to be at Mr. Pender's and nobody thought a bar would be a good place for a funeral gathering.

I remember Mr. Pender standing in the corner of Aunt Doris's kitchen. Jasper and Cordessa were huddled up in the living room, smoking cigarettes and playing in their plates of food. Everybody was gathered around them trying to attend to their needs. But Mr. Pender just stood in the corner, his big black hands in the pockets of his too-small brown church suit. One of his shoes was untied. His hair had been combed and

greased in the front, but the back looked lik
he'd been standing up against a wall all night. H
was the saddest person I'd ever seen because h
didn't have a way to bring his grief inside c
him. It just sat on his shoulders and clung to hi
arms and chest like a hand-me-down sweater
heavy and old. He couldn't seem to find a wa
to smooth it down or take it off. The loss of firs
his marriage and now his beloved child had cov
ered over his heart.

Mama took some cat-head biscuits and red
eye gravy, a gallon of tea, and some plastic silver
ware over to Aunt Doris's while everyone els
was at the service. But she didn't go to th
church, nor did she go by the east end of th
trailer park while Cordessa was there. Even now
all these years later, she's sort of like a fox havin
seen a fallen chicken feather when it comes t
Cordessa: she won't let it loose.